DEATH WAITED
AT RIALTO CREEK

This Large Print Book carries the
Seal of Approval of N.A.V.H.

DEATH WAITED
AT RIALTO CREEK

LEWIS B. PATTEN

THORNDIKE PRESS
A part of Gale, Cengage Learning

GALE
CENGAGE Learning·

Detroit • New York • San Francisco • New Haven, Conn • Waterville, Maine • London

GALE
CENGAGE Learning®

LIBRARY OF CONGRESS CATALOGING-IN-PUBLICATION DATA

Patten, Lewis B.
    Death waited at Rialto Creek / by Lewis B. Patten. — Large print ed.
    p. cm. — (Thorndike Press large print western)
    ISBN 978-1-4104-4645-9 (hardcover) — ISBN 1-4104-4645-X (hardcover)
    1. Large type books. I. Title.
    PS3566.A79D45 2012
    813'.54—dc23   2011048801

Published in 2012 by arrangement with Golden West Literary Agency.

Printed in Mexico
3 4 5 6 7 16 15 14 13

DEATH WAITED
AT RIALTO CREEK

CHAPTER 1

Dawn was a faint grey line above the undulating plain to eastward as Major Samuel Burkhalter put his horse down into the sandy bottom of Cut Nose Creek. He raised an arm, waved it forward, crossed the creek splashing, and climbed his horse out on the other side.

K Troop followed him. B Troop, under Lieutenant Hargreaves, waited in column of fours in the bottom of the creek, holding their prancing, nervous horses still. They were facing toward the northeast, and they leaned forward slightly, anticipating the signal that would send them forward in a charge.

Burkhalter rode unhurriedly, his men quietly walking their horses behind him. A guidon fluttered limply against the lightening sky. The major topped a low rise and halted, staring at the sleeping Cheyenne camp below him on the near bank of Cut

Nose Creek.

Again he raised an arm, beckoning and pointing on ahead. The troop passed him by twos, breaking off along the top of this low ridge, forming a line facing the Indian camp. The silence was broken only by the slight rattle of accoutrements, sometimes by the soft grunt of one of the waiting men. A sergeant cocked his carbine and afterward the sounds of other cocking carbines ran along the line, seemingly very loud in the quiet dawn.

Burkhalter drew his sabre, the steel sliding out of its scabbard with a distinctive, unmistakably hissing sound. He stood in his stirrups and leaned forward, eyes narrowed, face intent. His arm lifted and the sabre waved the line of men into motion, shrill cries so long held back now bursting from their lips. Burkhalter himself remained silent. His horse galloped down the long-tapering slope toward the nearest of the hide lodges and the air was suddenly filled with the crackling fire of a hundred guns.

Indians, rudely awakened by the shots and cries, by bullets ripping through the hide coverings above their heads, came stumbling dazedly from the tipis, some with weapons, some without, but all in various stages of nakedness. They began to fall before the withering hail of lead. Some turned to run, toward Cut Nose Creek, toward the temporary safety of its steep earthen banks.

But there was no safety for them there. Lieutenant Hargreaves led his howling troopers into sight, splashing water as high as a horseman's head. They laid a withering cross-fire into the lodges and into the half-dressed people trying to escape from them, their bullets making no distinctions as to age or sex.

Burkhalter's men swept on through the village, firing with pistols now, clubbing with rifle butts, slashing with sabres. At the bank of Cut Nose Creek they stopped, regrouped, then joined Hargreaves' men in a second charge back through the demoralised Indian camp.

Hargeaves took a bullet in the thigh and stared down at the gushing blood with disbelief, his face turned grey with shock. Private Shore tumbled from his saddle and was left behind, lying limp and blue amidst the shambles of the Cheyenne village, standing out sharply because of the colour of his uniform.

At the crest of the rise from which he had started only minutes before, Major Burkhalter halted his men and thereafter stared back down at the village lying mortally wounded on the bank of Cut Nose Creek. A ragged group of Indians was straggling away up the creek. A few of the wounded stirred. A minor-key death song lifted into the still air, putting gooseflesh on Burkhalter's arms. A child, somewhere, screamed shrilly and incessantly.

Burkhalter roared, "Burn it! Move in from this side and burn everything!"

Sergeant Hochstadt, his ordinarily red face somewhat pale, barked an order and half a dozen men moved cautiously down the slope toward the village edge. They dismounted and while two stood ready with carbines the other four found combustible material and began piling it against the tipi walls. One knelt and a moment later a plume of smoke rose into the still morning air.

Burkhalter shouted, "Sergeant, six men is not enough! Detail some more to help!"

Hochstadt nodded, neither looking at him nor speaking. He ordered more men to join the six and watched them ride away. Other plumes of smoke began to rise. A wounded Indian woman in one of the burning tipis began to scream monotonously.

A young trooper with a shock of straw-coloured hair and a face that looked greenish grey scrambled off his horse and bent double, vomiting. There was a rumble of subdued talk among the men, not distinguishable as to words. Lieutenant Hargreaves was lying on the grass fifty yards beyond the crest of the ridge. The surgeon was winding bandage around his wounded leg, from which the trouser had been cut away.

More Indians were now straggling away toward the creek. They disappeared over the edge of the steep cut-bank. Occasionally Burkhalter would catch movement upstream in the willows and heavy brush. They were funnelling off that way and it would be a simple thing to cut them off and annihilate them. No need for it, though. The village was wiped out. Fifty or sixty Indians lay dead down there. Fifty or sixty, of which more than half were men.

Burkhalter had sustained but two casualties, Lieutenant Hargreaves and Private Shore. That would look damned good in his report. He roared, "Sergeant Hochstadt! Take a detail and go through the lodges that have not been burned. I want all the white scalps you can find. I want pieces of clothing and trinkets that have belonged to settlers murdered by these savages!"

Hochstadt nodded. He barked out several names, then rode away downslope with

11

several troopers following him. The major said, "Sergeant Rounds!"

"Yes, sir?"

"Let the men dismount." Burkhalter turned his horse and rode to where Lieutenant Hargreaves was. "Can you ride, Jim?"

"Yes, sir." Hargreaves struggled to sit up but the surgeon pushed him back. "Lie still, Lieutenant. Do you want to bleed to death?"

"How soon can he leave, Dr. Lynch?"

"In a wagon — right away. He shouldn't ride a horse until to-morrow."

"Some of those savages got away. They could bring back reinforcements before to-morrow."

The surgeon didn't speak. The major turned his horse and rode back to the crest of the ridge.

The village was burning sluggishly now. There was still an occasional shot down there as one or another of the men finished off an Indian that wasn't dead.

Hochstadt came riding back at the head of his small detachment of men. They were loaded with souvenirs but they also carried scalps and assorted pieces of clothing either stolen from whites or traded from them legitimately. Burkhalter said, "Sergeant, send a man for the wagons. Lieutenant Hargreaves will not be able to ride. And have

12

Private Shore's body brought up here."

Hochstadt saluted. His blue eyes rested briefly on the major's face. He turned his head and spoke to one of the men and the trooper turned immediately and galloped his horse back in the direction from which they had come earlier. The supply wagons were only half a dozen miles away. They could get here in a couple of hours at most.

Burkhalter dismounted. His orderly had a fire going and a pot of coffee on. He poured a cup and brought it to the major. Burkhalter curtly acknowledged it. Sipping the scalding coffee, he stared at the blazing, dead village down below.

He had been brevet brigadier general during the last battles of the war but when peace came, he lost his rank. He had been assigned the permanent rank of major and he was still a major despite the fact that nearly five long years had passed.

He was ambitious and grimly determined to be a general again. But you don't get to be general in a miserable, god-forsaken outpost like Fort Kettering. Generals are made on the battlefield. Victories are the things that beget generals. The trouble was, before you can have a victory, you have to have a battle. And to have a battle, you have to have an enemy.

Well, now he had an enemy. The Cheyennes were his enemy. Enough of them had escaped to-day to carry the story of Cut Nose Creek to all the members of the tribe.

Back and forth he paced, back and forth, scowling at the smouldering tipis down below. The men came straggling back, the ones who had been detailed to fire it. The younger ones, those who had not served in the war, were pale.

The men built fires now. The sun was half-way up the sky. The smell of coffee and bacon filled the air. After a while the wagons rattled into sight.

By noon, the two troops were on their way back to Fort Kettering. Vultures appeared as tiny specks in the sky and soon were circling over the dead village on the bank of Cut Nose Creek.

Joe Moya rode in a comfortably relaxed, slouched position, reins in his left hand, lead rope of the pack animal in his right. He seemed almost to drowse, and perhaps he did sometimes, but there was little of the land or the sky that his indolent attention missed. He saw the vultures from a mile away as mere specks in the cloud-spotted sky. He saw the thin haze of smoke hanging over the valley of Cut Nose Creek where the village was.

Even so, alarm did not stir immediately in his mind. It was possible that some of the young men had gone on a hunt and had been unusually successful. That would account for the presence of the carrion-eating birds. The smoke? It seemed like more than a normal amount but perhaps it was just hanging there because there was no wind to carry it away.

Alarm did not stir immediately in his mind, yet something stirred in his instincts, something that made a light, puzzled frown appear on his impassive face, that made his narrowed eyes narrow even more. He touched heels lightly to his horse's sides and the animal broke into a sluggish trot.

Joe was a thick-set man of medium height. His black hair was long, like that of an Indian, but not braided the way an Indian's was. His face was dark, roughened by sun and wind, clean-shaven except for a thick moustache spreading out on both sides of his mouth.

Joe Moya's eyes were the things about him that men remembered long after he was gone. Most times they seemed like mere slits, with very little of the eyes showing between the lids. But what did show of those eyes was blue, and cold, and somehow unnerving, as though Joe Moya possessed the capability of looking beyond a man's façade clear to the depths of his soul.

He did not, of course. Joe Moya was a simple man, an uneducated man. He could write his own name, laboriously and carefully, but that was all that he *could* write.

Nor could he read, not the written word at least. The things Joe Moya read were the words that men and animals wrote upon the land. These things he could read in spite of the effort of wind and weather to obscure their meanings from his eyes.

The closer he got to the village on Cut Nose Creek, the deeper his frown became. And the closer he got, the more he urged his horse to greater speed until at last, when he topped the final rise and looked down, his horse was travelling at a run, forced onward by an angry, impatient quirt.

He hauled the animal to a startled halt. He stared at the village, at the fires that still smouldered lazily, at the bodies lying sprawled on the ground and in the bed of Cut Nose Creek. There was a sudden hollowness in Joe Moya's gut. There was tightness in his chest, as though giant hands were squeezing it. His breath came in shallow gusts. His face was twisted, as though from actual, physical pain almost beyond his ability to endure.

16

A wordless groan escaped his mouth. His heels drummed on the horse's sides and the quirt rose and fell savagely. The startled animal leaped ahead. . . .

The packhorse followed more slowly, his head to one side so that he wouldn't step on the dropped halter rope.

Joe rode like a man who knew exactly where he was, who knew exactly where he was going. He pounded up out of Cut Nose Creek, past bodies his eyes were almost afraid to touch, and on to a certain lodge, also smouldering but not yet burned all the way to the ground.

He left his horse in a running leap, the way a great mountain cat leaves his perch on a low, horizontal limb. He plunged into the lodge, disdaining the smoke, disdaining the fire that crackled yet on the far side of it. He threw himself down beside the inert body of the young Cheyenne woman and laid his head against her left breast, listening. . . .

Three times he shifted his head, three times listened once again. When he finally raised it, tears were running silently from his eyes, silently coursing across his weathered cheeks.

He sat there for a long time, staring into her face. Its expression was peaceful and the eyes were closed. He rubbed dazedly at the blood on his ear and cheek, blood that had rubbed off on him when he laid his head against her breast. The tears continued to flow silently from his eyes, to run across his cheeks and to drop unheeded to the earthen floor.

He began to cough from the pall of smoke within the lodge. He got to his feet and his eyes searched the place, settling on two smaller bodies lying on a pile of smouldering robes at the far side of it. He crossed to them swiftly and pulled them clear of the smoking robes. He picked up the larger one in his arms, carried the body outside, and laid it gently on the ground.

He returned for the smaller one, coughing, tears streaming from his eyes. He carried this one out and returned for the woman.

When all three had been laid side by side on the ground outside the lodge, he knelt and put his head against the children's chests, first that of the girl, then that of the boy. When he again raised his head, his eyes were bleak, his face numb with shock. He stared emptily, almost unseeingly, at the three. This was his family, Red Earth Woman, his wife. Little Squirrel, his son. Laughing Girl, his daughter. This was his family and all were dead. Dead in a savage, senseless massacre.

He stumbled dazedly to his feet. He walked through the village, reading the things written on the ground. He climbed the slope and at the crest of the low ridge cast back and forth, reading also the sign that was here, storing the things he discovered in his mind. When he walked back down the hill he knew where the troops were from and who their commanding officer was. He knew what time of day they had struck because dew had been on the ground when the first tracks were made. He knew how many there had been and he knew one had been wounded and had bled heavily. He knew further that one had been killed, brought to the crest of the ridge on horseback where he had been transferred to a wagon for the trip back to Fort Kettering.

He went into the lodge and rummaged around among his things until he found a short-handled miner's shovel. Going back outside, he lifted his wife and carried her upstream from the village until he found a pretty spot to bury her. He laid her down and returned for the children. When all three had been brought to this place, he began to dig.

He worked steadily, tirelessly. He worked

until long after the sun had dropped below the horizon in the west. By moonlight, he placed the bodies gently in the graves, and by moonlight filled them in. Exhausted now, he slept beside the graves with his horses picketed nearby.

At dawn he was awake. At dawn he mounted his horse and rode out toward Fort Kettering, trailing the packhorse behind.

His face was once more impassive, his eyes mere slits against the slanting, blinding rays of the rising sun. He rode at a steady, unhurried walk. One man cannot, in a day, revenge himself against a hundred and sixty men. It was going to take some time. But Joe Moya had the time. Time was all that he had left.

CHAPTER 2

The paymaster's wagon lurched noisily along the narrow, two-track road. Up on the seat, sometimes falling against the trooper driving, Captain Wilhite dozed. Two troopers rode in front of the light wagon, two more behind. Lieutenant Martin Keefe, under orders transferring him to Fort Kettering, brought up the rear, his face sombre, his eyes narrowed against the dust and now-hanging sun.

To Keefe's right, the Platte flowed sluggishly, lined with cottonwoods and willows, sometimes spreading out behind beaver dams to form irregular, placid ponds. Several times flights of ducks whirred overhead and descended, quacking noisily, toward the water fifty feet below.

North of the river, the land was relatively flat, reaching out into hazy distances, but on this side was a bluff and a ragged spine of low, sagebrush-covered hills, through which the road wound like a snake.

Fort Kettering came into sight half an hour before sundown and at his first glimpse of it, Lieutenant Keefe involuntarily tightened his reins and stopped his horse.

He was a big young man, his features seeming unfinished and rough. His eyes, beneath brows unusually shaggy for a man so young, were blue, or grey, depending on the light and right now they had a cautious wariness to them.

There was reason for his wariness. The commanding officer at Fort Kettering was Major Samuel Burkhalter. The same Samuel Burkhalter who had, during the war, falsely accused Keefe's father of foot-dragging in the battle of Indian Creek. And because the newspapers had managed to get hold of the story, because they had apparently believed Burkhalter instead of Keefe, Martin Keefe's father had been forced to resign his commission and had died a year later, bitter and discredited and unable to vindicate himself or even to fight the shadows that had ruined him.

There had been no way to prove Burkhalter had given the story to the newspapers. There had been no way to prove Burkhalter had attacked before the appointed time, trying to hog the glory for himself. A good many of those who might have disproved Burkhalter's claims of innocence were dead, the others afraid to talk. Subordinates simply do not accuse such a famous soldier of lying — not if they value their own military careers. Besides, there had been no court-martial, no hearing of any kind. The whole case was tried in the newspapers and by word of mouth. It was deemed not in the best interests of the Army to have a public trial.

Keefe stared sombrely at the squarish, adobe fort. He had requested assignment to this place and he had not revealed his personal animosity toward Samuel Burkhalter. Now he wondered why. Was it because he intended to revenge himself against the man? He shook his head. No. His father would not have wanted that and he did not want it himself. At least he didn't think he did.

Perhaps it was a kind of morbid curiosity that had brought him here. Perhaps he just wanted to know Burkhalter and to observe the man. Perhaps he had some idea of proving his father's story enough to justify reopening the case. He shook his head with sudden impatience at his own foolishness. He urged his horse into a trot and caught up with the paymaster's wagon a quarter mile from the fort.

Built mainly of adobe, the fort blended into its surroundings admirably. Its colour was the colour of the bluff. At two diagonal corners were lookout towers perhaps eight feet higher than the walls.

The main gate, of three-inch planks, was weathered grey. It swung open to admit the paymaster's detail, which Keefe followed into the fort.

What buildings there were at Fort Kettering were located against the walls, utilising the wall of the fort as the rear building wall. In a rectangular shape, Kettering was more than two hundred yards long, ninety yards wide. Nearest the gate, along the north wall, were the bachelor officers' quarters and, adjoining, the two-story married officers' quarters. Next was battalion headquarters and the officers' mess, next to that a line of store and supply rooms, and beyond that, the sutler's store. Adjoining the sutler's store was the post hospital and the guardhouse.

At the west end of the compound, beginning next to the guardhouse, were hay storage barns, and a granary, and beyond that, the stables and corrals and the blacksmith's shop. In the southwest corner was a rather large lean-to shed, in which various vehicles were stored — supply wagons, ambulances, even a buggy for the use of the officers' wives. The south wall was taken up by enlisted men's barracks and by the enlisted men's mess hall and kitchen, but most of the area directly opposite the officers' quarters was clear.

The flagpole was in the centre of the parade ground. Right now a squad of men marched back and forth to the sharp commands of a corporal. Men receiving extra duty in the form of drill as punishment, Keefe thought fleetingly, knowing there is nothing a cavalryman hates worse than infantry drill.

Captain Wilhite descended from the paymaster's wagon in front of the battalion headquarters. The two troopers at the rear dismounted. While one held the horses, the other dragged a heavy strongbox from the wagon and carried it inside. Troopers and wagon moved away toward the stables. Lieutenant Keefe dismounted and handed his horse's reins to a trooper who came from headquarters and saluted him.

He crossed the narrow, pole-supported gallery and stepped inside, colliding violently with a woman in the act of trying to step outside. He had a fleeting impression of softness, of an elusive perfume, of a wisp of hair tickling his nose. Then he was holding her arms with both hands firmly to steady her, and feeling the heat of an embarrassed flush mounting into his face. Before he could speak, he heard her say, "You can release me now, Lieutenant. I do not think I am going to fall."

Lieutenant Keefe let his arms drop to his sides. He felt a touch of irritation because her composure was greater than his own and murmured, "Sorry, ma'am. That was clumsy of me. I hope that you're not hurt."

His eyes were now more accustomed to the dim light and he could see her features clearly for the first time. Seeing them, he felt a shock that was almost physical. For an instant he stared, then once again felt his embarrassment mount.

She was a small-statured woman, but she was not slight. Her hair was a deep, rich brown that just missed being black. She wore it in a mass of curls at the nape of her neck. Her skin was like flawless ivory and her eyes were a startling shade of grey. Her mouth, with lips slightly parted by surprise, was firm and soft. She made a sudden smile, her eyes studying him with a singular lack of embarrassment. "No, Lieutenant. I am not hurt. Good day." She brushed past him and was gone and he could hear her light footfalls fading along the adobe gallery.

He turned his attention to a captain standing in an open office doorway across the room. He saluted. "Lieutenant Keefe reporting, sir." He reached into his tunic pocket and removed his papers. He crossed the room and handed them to the other officer.

The captain was a short, stocky man — a greying man with bushy sideburns giving him a broad-faced look. He scanned the papers briefly and handed them back to Keefe. "I'm Captain MacPhee, Lieutenant. Came with the paymaster's detail, did you?"

"Yes, sir."

"And you've met Mrs. Burkhalter."

Keefe stared briefly, unbelievingly, then abruptly lowered his glance. "Yes, sir. I guess I have."

"And you know Captain Wilhite, the paymaster. The corporal here is Ord, Daniel Ord."

Keefe nodded, first at the paymaster, then at the corporal, who saluted perfunctorily.

"The corporal will show you to your quarters, Lieutenant Keefe."

"Thank you."

MacPhee said, "Put him in with Lieutenant Hargreaves, Corporal."

"Yes, sir." Ord glanced at Keefe. "Come with me, Lieutenant. Did you have a bag or trunk or anything?"

"A carpetbag and a box. They're in the paymaster's wagon."

"I'll have them brought over to you." Ord went outside onto the cool gallery and Keefe followed him. A breeze had come up, blowing from the river below the bluff. The sun was down, but high, puffy clouds in the sky flamed brilliant orange in its dying glow. There was a light smell of dust in the air, and the smell of frying meat, and the ever present, pungent smell of the sagebrush beyond the walls.

The corporal walked silently ahead of Keefe in the direction of the gate. There seemed to be no separate buildings here, just one long one, with doors and windows opening onto the gallery. Ord stopped in front of one of the doors and opened it. Striking a match, he went inside. He lighted a lamp, trimmed the wick, and turned. "I'll have your things brought up right away."

"Thank you, Corporal." Keefe hesitated a moment, then asked, "Where is Major Burkhalter, Corporal?"

"Out on patrol, sir. He was supposed to be back to-night."

Keefe nodded and the corporal went out, pulling the door closed after him. Keefe heard his steps fade along the gallery.

He stared around the room. The walls were of adobe, whitewashed but very rough. The ceiling was supported by peeled pine poles. Seeing a doorway opening into another room, he crossed to it and looked inside. There was a bed and a desk and a chair. There was a commode, the top of which apparently served as a washstand too. The furniture was almost identical with that in the room where Keefe stood. A man's personal things were strewn carelessly about and there were a few photographs. Keefe turned, sat down on the bed, and stared at the four bare walls.

He was used to austere surroundings but this was even more austere than most. The floor was of swept adobe brick, uneven and rough. There was a block of wood under one leg of the bed to level it.

Suddenly he found himself thinking of Mrs. Burkhalter, with whom he had collided so violently. His senses remembered the softness, the elusive fragrance, the tickling wisp of hair. He was remembering too the quality of her voice, the way her eyes had studied him.

Burkhalter's wife. It seemed unthinkable. Burkhalter must be near the age Keefe's father would have been if he had lived. But Mrs. Burkhalter was no more than twenty-five. He was sure of that.

He put her from his mind determinedly. He had no business thinking about the wife of the commandant, particularly thinking about her in this way. He had troubles enough, coming here to serve under a man he hated, who would hate him too when he realised who he was.

He heard steps approaching along the gallery and a moment later there was a knock upon the door. He said, "Come in," and Corporal Ord came in, carrying Keefe's bulky carpetbag. He was followed by a private, carrying a wooden box. Keefe said, "Thank you, Corporal," and Ord and the other man withdrew, leaving the door ajar.

Keefe stepped outside. He stood briefly in

the yellow lamplight streaming from the door while he withdrew a thin cigar from the pocket of his tunic. He bit off the end and struck a match. He lighted it and puffed pleasurably.

He stared through gathering dusk toward the gate, then turned his glance in the other direction toward headquarters. He caught a movement farther along the gallery and saw a woman step out onto it. She glanced in his direction, then went quickly back inside. He thought the woman had been Mrs. Burkhalter but the light had been too poor to tell for sure.

He frowned. The picture of her that he carried in his mind was vivid and had not faded in the least. He heard shouts outside the gates, heard them squeak as the sentries opened them. He heard the familiar sounds of a mounted troop and saw the first of them ride in. When all were inside, they executed a "left by twos" at the command of an officer, and were quickly dismissed. They rode away raggedly in the direction of the stables.

Keefe heard a door down the gallery and saw Burkhalter's wife come out again. She stood in the lamplight streaming from the door, waiting.

There was noise and confusion in the

compound, men shouting back and forth, a bugle tuning up for mess call. Keefe could hear the murmur of voices as Burkhalter and his wife conversed briefly before stepping into their house. He wished he could have seen Burkhalter more clearly than he had. He did not, frankly, remember the man at all. He had only seen him once and that had been more than five years ago.

He watched the ambulance driven to the post hospital, and watched two stretchers lifted out and carried in. There had been trouble, then, and two casualties. He was faintly surprised because he had not known there was trouble on the plains.

A man came walking wearily along the gallery toward him. He stopped short of Keefe and peered through the darkness at his face. He said, "Heard there was a new man. I'm the surgeon, Lynch." He stuck out a hand and Keefe took it, finding it rough and stubby but very strong. He said, "Lieutenant Keefe, sir. They put me in here with Lieutenant Hargreaves. I suppose he'll be along rather soon."

Lynch shook his head. "Not for a while, Keefe. Hargreaves caught a bullet back there on Cut Nose Creek. Thigh. He bled a lot."

"There *was* trouble, then. I had thought

31

the plains tribes were peaceful, sir."

"They were, Keefe, but they're not peaceful any more."

Keefe was puzzled by the reply but he did not press for an explanation. He could see that Dr. Lynch was tired. Lynch murmured something about being glad to have met him and went on, disappearing into the room next along the gallery. A moment later a lamp flickered alight inside the room, throwing a faint glow through the small front windows onto the gallery.

Nervousness touched Lieutenant Keefe. He went into his room, poured water from the pitcher on the washstand into the basin, then got razor, strop, soap, and brush from his bag. He washed and shaved, then replaced and brushed his tunic, and relighted his cigar, which had gone out. Blowing out the lamp, he left the room. His cigar made a spot of reddish light on the dark gallery. The smoke drifted down the gallery on the breeze.

Keefe walked slowly toward the gate. He was hungry but he didn't want to be the first man to show up at the officers' mess. He reached the gate and acknowledged the salute of the sentry guarding it. Above and beyond he could see another man on the platform of the lookout tower. He turned to go but stopped when a voice yelled from outside the gate, "It's Joe Moya, trooper. Open up and let me in."

The gate swung back and the horseman rode through it into the fort, trailing a packhorse behind. Seeing Keefe, he stopped. He did not dismount, nor did he salute. He said, "Guess I don't know you, Lieutenant. I'm Joe Moya. I thought the major might be lookin' for civilian scouts."

Keefe reached up a hand. Moya's was big and incredibly strong. Keefe said, "I just arrived this evening, Mr. Moya, with the paymaster's detail. I expect you know where the major's quarters are."

"I know. But I'll wait until morning to talk to him." Moya rode away, disappearing into the darkness in the direction of the stables at the far end of the fort.

Frowning, Keefe followed him. Something about Moya had bothered him. He walked toward the officers' mess but he came to no conclusions as to what it had been about Moya that had troubled him. It was too vague, too elusive a something to have a name put to it.

He stepped into the adobe-walled, whitewashed room with its long table and many chairs, prepared to meet his fellow officers. Captain MacPhee saw him and advanced with a friendly smile. But Keefe did not miss the worried concern in the captain's eyes, concern that had not been there before Burkhalter brought his troops back into the fort.

CHAPTER 3

MacPhee was a warm and friendly man. He said, "Come on, Keefe. I'll introduce you." He put his hand on Keefe's shoulder and guided him toward the others, grouped companionably in the centre of the room. He said, "We have three troops here, Lieutenant, B, K, and L. I command L Troop, Lieutenant Hargreaves, who is senior lieutenant, commands B, and Captain Leighton commands K."

Keefe didn't recall seeing any officers with the two returning troops except for Burkhalter and the surgeon but he didn't comment on it. He was shaking hands with Captain Leighton, a short-statured, balding man and after that with Lieutenant Mills, boyish-faced and several years younger than himself. Another lieutenant, whom MacPhee introduced as Lieutenant DuBois, was a dark, thin-faced man about his own age. The surgeon took Keefe's hand, gripped it, and said, smiling, "We've already introduced ourselves. Are you getting settled in, Lieutenant Keefe?"

Keefe shook his head. "Not yet, sir."

The surgeon looked at Mills. "How's Catherine, Lieutenant?"

Mills forced a smile. "There is not much change, Dr. Lynch. I'd appreciate it if you'd look in on her."

"Certainly. Immediately after we finish here."

The paymaster, Captain Wilhite, came in and they gathered around the table and sat down. A white-aproned trooper began to carry in the food. Keefe had never eaten venison and found it delicious, if somewhat richer than beef. For dessert there was dried apple pie, and after that coffee. Several of the men lighted cigars. The trooper cleared the table and withdrew. MacPhee looked at the surgeon, his eyes blue and very sharp. "What happened out there, Dr. Lynch?"

The surgeon hesitated but only for a moment. "We attacked a sleeping village and slaughtered them. Hargreaves caught a bullet in the thigh and Private Shore was killed. That's all there is."

Leighton grunted sourly through a blue cloud of smoke, "I'd say it was quite enough. How many Indians were killed?"

"I didn't count. Fifty or sixty I would suppose."

Leighton whistled. "There'll be hell to pay."

MacPhee said softly, "Maybe that's just what he wants."

Leighton asked, "How is he going to justify it?"

The surgeon said, "There were white scalps in the lodges and various odds and ends of clothing whose owners were originally white. He had these things gathered up and brought them back with him as evidence."

Captain Wilhite stood up. "If you'll excuse me, gentlemen." His voice was cool with disapproval. MacPhee stared at him, his expression holding a touch of irritation at Wilhite's pompousness. At last he said deliberately, "You may not approve of this discussion, Captain, but what has happened will make your job no easier. You may find that from now on four troopers or forty will not be enough to safely escort you."

Wilhite's expression did not soften. He nodded his head curtly, went to the door, and stepped out onto the gallery.

Dr. Lynch stood up. "Come along, Mills. We'll go take a look at Catherine." He went out, followed by Lieutenant Mills.

Now there was a certain awkwardness in the room and an apparent disinclination to carry the discussion farther. MacPhee, in an obvious attempt to change the subject, stared thoughtfully at Keefe. "I seem to recall the name Keefe, Lieutenant. Have I served with you before?"

Keefe shook his head. "I doubt it, Captain. I'm sure I would have remembered you."

"The name's familiar." MacPhee frowned with his attempt to recall his connection with the name. Suddenly he glanced sharply at Keefe. "I have it. There was a Colonel Keefe at Indian Creek."

"My father, Captain."

"Yes." The silence was awkward. For an instant, Keefe hesitated. Then he got to his feet. "I believe I will try to get unpacked tonight." He nodded at the group, turned, and left the room. He went out onto the gallery, conscious of the silence he left behind. He pulled the door firmly closed and walked along the gallery.

MacPhee whistled soundlessly. "Got my foot in it that time, didn't I? I didn't make the connection at first. I was just being polite."

DuBois asked, "What happened at Indian Creek?"

MacPhee frowned. "It was in the newspapers. Quite a scandal at the time. Major Burkhalter was a part of it and so was Colonel Keefe. Burkhalter was brevet colonel at the time. Made general shortly afterward." He pulled thoughtfully at his cigar. After a moment he went on, "As I remember it, the Rebs were dug in on a bluff overlooking Indian Creek. A two-pronged offensive was planned, Burkhalter to attack from one side, Keefe from the other. Burkhalter said Keefe delayed beyond the appointed time. Anyway, he attacked and the Rebs slaughtered him. He took the bluff but the cost was terrible. Keefe claimed Burkhalter attacked before the time agreed upon but, frankly, his defence sounded pretty weak coming on the heels of Burkhalter's claim to the contrary. Keefe resigned not long afterward and died within a year."

"And now his son is here to serve under Burkhalter," said Leighton softly. "What do you make of that?"

"Make of it? I don't know. It's probably just a coincidence."

"Think Major Burkhalter will make the connection, MacPhee?"

"Of course he will, though I doubt he'll mention it."

"What do you really think about the battle of Indian Creek? Do you think Burkhalter told the truth, or Keefe?"

MacPhee smiled. "I don't think about such things. Burkhalter is my commanding officer and Indian Creek was a long, long time ago." He got up and pushed his chair under the table and out of the way. "Good night, Ralph." He nodded at Leighton, and at DuBois, crossed to the door, and stepped out into the night.

He stood there motionless on the gallery for several moments, his face sombre, his body relaxed and loose. He was thinking of Martha Burkhalter and of her collision earlier this afternoon with Lieutenant Keefe. He had not missed the almost speculative way she had studied Keefe and now he frowned, remembering that. He turned and stepped out onto the parade, afterward pacing deliberately toward the gate.

The guard beside it, Private Schulte of L Troop, sprang to attention and MacPhee acknowledged his salute. A half-moon hung low in the western sky, and MacPhee commented, "Nice evening, Private Schulte."

"Yes, sir." The man was silent a moment and then he said, "We admitted Joe Moya a while ago, Captain. I expect you'll find him at the sutler's store if you want to talk to him."

MacPhee nodded. He wasn't surprised

that Joe Moya was here. Word of trouble on the plains travelled fast. Moya would be looking for work and Burkhalter would undoubtedly hire him. Moya was a good scout — one of the best.

He returned across the empty parade ground toward headquarters. There was a lamp burning inside and he went in. Corporal Ord was there. His chair was tilted back and he was reading a tattered Kansas City newspaper. He brought his chair forward and sat up straight but MacPhee said impatiently, "At ease, Corporal. As you were," and the corporal returned his attention to the newspaper.

MacPhee went into his office, lighted the lamp, and sat down. He blew a cloud of smoke at the lamp and watched it eddy with the rising heat from the chimney. A light frown stayed on his face.

He wished he could understand his uneasiness. He tried to rationalise it and discovered it was the result of three unconnected things that had happened this afternoon. The first had been Keefe's arrival at the fort and the immediate interest Martha Burkhalter had shown in him. The second was Burkhalter's return and the revelation that he had attacked and wiped out the Cheyenne village on Cut Nose Creek. The third was learning that Keefe was the son of Colonel Keefe, one of the principals in the scandal over the battle of Indian Creek.

Three things, any one of which could be explosive enough even by itself. Combined they could . . . He shook his head impatiently. He was imagining things. Why should Keefe's presence here threaten trouble? It was ridiculous and melodramatic to suppose he was here for purposes of revenge and he was surely mature enough to stay clear of the commandant's wife.

As for the attack at Cut Nose Creek . . . that could make trouble and it was certain that it would. There would be action in the coming days. They would take the field again — against the Cheyenne and probably against the Arapaho as well. He wondered if the Sioux would get into it and decided that would depend on how much the conflict spread.

It angered him to think how unnecessary it was. It angered him to think of Private Shore lying dead on a slab in the post hospital, of Hargreaves with a bullet in his thigh. It angered him even more to think of the others who would die in the months to come.

He understood why Burkhalter had attacked the village on Cut Nose Creek.

Burkhalter wanted to be a general again. He had decided this was the only way.

MacPhee had been puzzled a week ago when Burkhalter took K Troop and B Troop out, leaving all the officers but Hargreaves and Dr. Lynch behind. Now he wasn't puzzled any more. Burkhalter had known what he intended to do when he rode away from the fort. He'd left most of the other officers behind because he didn't want any arguments.

MacPhee blew out the lamp. He went outside and stood on the gallery, staring into the night. On a nearby ridge, a coyote yelped and was joined by several more. MacPhee wondered idly if there were Indians just outside the walls.

It was possible, he decided, but it was probably a little soon. He'd issue orders in the morning, though, about the men going outside the walls.

Thoughtfully, he paced back and forth along the gallery, frowning to himself.

CHAPTER 4

Morning came cool and misty out of the east, the sun shining weakly through the haze rising like smoke from the meandering Platte. A meadowlark trilled with clear sweetness outside the walls, to be answered by another and by another still.

Morning brought smells absent throughout the remainder of the day. The sage was stronger and more pungent because dew had wet its blue-green leaves. There were the smells of earth and of other growing things and there were also the ever present smells of the fort itself, the smells of hay and grain and corrals, the smells of leather and horses, of wood smoke and of coffee brewing in the kitchen adjoining the enlisted men's mess.

Washed and shaved and with trousers and tunic carefully brushed, Lieutenant Keefe stepped out of his quarters at a little after six. The sun was blinding now, slanting out of the east and bathing the gallery with its brilliance, having risen above the river's morning mist. Keefe took a long, deep breath and remembered Mrs. Burkhalter, the commandant's wife. He remembered too who Burkhalter was, the man who had ruined his father and caused his death.

He walked briskly along the gallery past the Burkhalters' closed door and beyond until he reached the officers' mess.

There was a pitcher of coffee on the table, and cups, and sugar. He poured himself coffee, nodding and smiling at Captain Leighton and at Lieutenant DuBois, who were already there.

Sipping the coffee, he crossed to them in time to hear DuBois ask, "What will happen now?"

"He'll send scouts out and learn where their villages are. He'll attack them again and again wherever they may be. It will be a long and brutal war but ultimately the Government will designate reservations for them and order them confined as they have with other tribes. They will go to their reservations and that will be the end of the Indian wars. Those involving the Cheyennes at least."

"And Major Burkhalter will be a general."

A voice from the door asked, "Did I hear my name?"

Keefe turned his head. Lieutenant DuBois flushed with embarrassment but he did not evade. "Yes, sir. We were discussing the action that you were in. We were speculating as to what might happen next."

Burkhalter stared closely at DuBois, a frown on his heavy face. He was a big man, over six feet tall and broad of shoulder. His upper body was grossly overweight and looked like a barrel tightly encased in the blue tunic of the cavalry.

He wore a moustache, a flowing, cavalry-style moustache that curled upward at its ends and was lightly waxed. He wore his hair rather long in a style that would not have been permitted in a younger officer. His face was florid, seemingly from a collar too tight for him. There was a network of fine, dark red veins on both his weathered cheeks. His eyes were brown, and very hard, which impression may have been caused by the way they were narrowed now. Lines at the corners of his eyes, crow's-feet lines, would have softened another face. They only made Burkhalter's seem more harsh.

Without commenting, Burkhalter shifted his glance to Keefe. Keefe brought his hand up in a salute. "Lieutenant Keefe, sir. I arrived with the paymaster's detail last evening. I did not report to you last night because I guessed you would be tired."

Burkhalter saluted perfunctorily, then extended his hand. Keefe took it and found the grip strong, perhaps more so than was necessary. He thought fleetingly that a man can tell a great deal about another man simply by shaking hands with him. Men who are weak and diffident have weakly diffident grips. Men who feel a need to prove something usually have unusually strong handclasps. Burkhalter would, superficially at least, seem to be one of these. The major said, "Bring your papers to headquarters after breakfast, Keefe." He walked to the table and poured himself coffee. He turned and Keefe felt his eyes steadily studying him.

"He's made the connection," he thought. "He knows who I am." He turned his head and met Burkhalter's steady regard with an equally steady glance and derived mild satisfaction from seeing Burkhalter look away. But he did not miss the flush that rose to Burkhalter's face afterward and he thought, "I've angered him," surprised that it had been so easy for him to do. Frowning faintly to himself, he walked to the window and stared out at the sun-washed parade.

Burkhalter remained apart, aloof, until Dr. Lynch, the surgeon, arrived, and after that the two walked to the far end of the room where they stood conversing in subdued tones, presumably about Hargreaves's wound. Others entered and joined the larger group.

A trooper in a white apron put a white cloth on the table, set it, and brought in the food — fried potatoes, fried venison, hot biscuits, honey, and gravy. The men gathered around the table and sat down. Burkhalter took the place at the head of the table. He looked at his officers one by one.

He said, "You have no doubt been speculating about the action K and B Troops saw the day before yesterday. I shall make it clear to you. We attacked a village on Cut Nose Creek at dawn with decisive results. Fifty or sixty Indians were killed. The village was destroyed. Certain items were found which proved to my complete satisfaction that these Indians have been engaged in murdering settlers and in plundering their homes."

He paused for an instant. The room was utterly silent, the only sounds being a faint clattering of pots from the direction of the kitchen. Burkhalter went on, "I intend to send out scouts to-day to determine where the hostiles are encamped. When we learn that, we shall attack them again and again wherever they are. I intend to put a stop to the outrages they have been committing against white settlers once and for all. Perhaps in so doing, we shall be instrumental in pacifying this frontier."

No one spoke. Burkhalter picked up his knife and fork. "I suggest you eat, gentlemen, before your food gets cold."

Talk thereafter was subdued and self-conscious. Keefe was glad when the meal was over with. He walked briskly along the gallery to his quarters. When he emerged again he had his papers in his hand. He walked directly to headquarters and went inside. Another corporal was on duty this morning at the desk. He looked up, said, "Major Burkhalter said you were to come on in, sir," and gestured toward a door on which the word "Commandant" was painted in gold.

Keefe crossed to the door and knocked. Burkhalter's voice ordered him to come in. He entered, closed the door, crossed to the desk, and handed his transfer papers to Burkhalter.

Burkhalter scanned them carefully. "The name Keefe is familiar, Lieutenant," he said without looking up.

"Yes, sir. My father was Colonel Rufus Keefe. I believe he served with you during the late war between the states."

Burkhalter glanced up now, his eyes like ice. "You know very well that he served with me. You also know that I was responsible for his resignation and disgrace."

Keefe felt his face go white. He said, "Yes, sir. I do know that."

"Why are you here, Lieutenant? There are a hundred other commands where you would not be required to serve under a man you hate."

"I didn't say I hated you, sir. I'm not even

sure I do."

Burkhalter studied him. "You're quartered with Hargreaves, are you not?"

"Yes, sir."

"Very well, Lieutenant. You may go. You will be assigned to L Troop under Captain MacPhee."

"Very good, sir." Keefe saluted, turned smartly on his heel, and left. His face reddened as he stepped out of headquarters onto the gallery. Burkhalter had made him feel like a schoolboy, intentionally, he was sure. He was angry, but it was helpless anger which nothing was going to ease. In fairness, he had to admit Burkhalter had made no more of his relationship with his father than was necessary. Neither had he evaded the relationship.

Yet Keefe was now absolutely certain of one thing, if he had not been sure before. Burkhalter had attacked too soon at Indian Creek, trying to hog the glory for himself. Keeefe didn't know why he was so sure but he was.

Nor had Burkhalter changed. He was still willing to sacrifice lives upon the altar of personal advancement. His attack at Cut Nose Creek proved that if, indeed, proof was necessary. Keefe stood outside head-quarters for a moment, staring at the paymaster's wagon being drawn into place in front of the barracks across the way. He heard pay call blown by a bugler with only a small part of his mind. Almost like a sleepwalker, he turned and made his way along the gallery.

Joe Moya spent the night in a tiny room opening off the main room of the sutler's store. He could have slept in the barracks with the enlisted men or he could have had an empty room in the bachelor officers' quarters, of which there were several since the garrison was undermanned. But he preferred it here. This place felt more civilian than any other within the fort, with its liquor smell, its tobacco smoke smell, its smell of the goods that lined the sutler's shelves and of food cooking in the tiny kitchen at the rear. A man could always get something to eat here if he was willing to pay for it.

But most of all, Joe Moya doubted if he could go along with the good-natured give and take of a bunch of soldiers now. Not since day before yesterday. Not since he'd seen what they had done at Cut Nose Creek.

This morning he sat on the edge of the bed a moment, staring at the floor, running his fingers through his hair. It wasn't going to be easy for him, going to Burkhalter and asking for a job. It wasn't going to be easy hiding the virulence of his hate, or controlling himself when what he wanted most was to kill the man outright.

But he *would* control himself because he wanted more than Burkhalter's death. The dead bodies of his family cried out for more than simple revenge against Fort Kettering's commanding officer.

He pulled on his boots and went out into the store. There was a lone trooper at the bar, apparently getting himself an eye-opener to ease last night's hangover. Moya thought absently that there'd be a hell of a lot more hangovers to-morrow morning than there were to-day. The paymaster would see to that.

He went into the kitchen. A Mexican woman, fat and middle-aged, turned her head and looked at him impassively. He said, "Cook me up something. I don't care what it is. I'll have some coffee now."

He went out and sat down at a table near the end of the bar. After a moment the woman brought him a thick mug filled with coffee and put it down in front of him. The trooper stared at him owlishly, then turned and left.

Moya drank the coffee. He got up and went out the back door into a little courtyard jammed up against the outside wall. There was a pump here, and on a rickety table, a bar of soap and a dirty towel. Moya pumped cold water over his head, lathered, rinsed, and dried himself on the towel. He ran a piece of comb through his hair, rubbed the black stubble on his face reflectively, then went back inside.

There was a plate of food on the table beside his coffee cup, which had been refilled. He ate, hardly aware of what he ate, and when he had finished paid for the food, went out, and walked steadily toward headquarters.

He sat down on the edge of one of the straight-backed chairs while he waited for Major Burkhalter to call him in. When Burkhalter did, he got up and went in, walking like a cat, feeling out of place. Burkhalter motioned to a chair and Joe sat down.

Wasting no time on amenities, he said, "Figured you might be lookin' fer scouts." He had never worked for Burkhalter, but he had met the man. Burkhalter now studied him, scowling, and finally said, "I have heard you have an Indian wife. Cheyenne, isn't she?"

Moya met his glance steadily and unwaveringly. He said, "Wife ain't exactly the right word, Major. Man needs a woman, be

52

she Injun or white, an' he takes what he can get."

The answer seemed to satisfy Burkhalter. The door opened and a trooper put his head inside the door. "O'Rourke is out here, Major. Want me to send him in?"

Burkhalter nodded. The trooper withdrew and a moment later an oldish man came in, a man with long grey hair and a stained grey beard, with skin like dark-tanned leather and eyes that were blue but beginning to be less sharp than they once had been. He nodded at Moya. "Hallo, Joe. Heard you was here." O'Rourke glanced at the major. "Send for me, Major?"

"Yes. I want you both. One of you can sweep everything north of the river, and the other everything to the south. I want to know where their villages are and I want to know their strength. I want to know if they're on the move, and if so where they're headed. I want both of you back within a week."

Moya had been watching O'Rourke. He wondered if O'Rourke knew any more about his connection with the Cheyennes than Burkhalter had. If O'Rourke spilled anything about his Cheyenne family and if Burkhalter learned they had been killed at Cut Nose Creek . . .

O'Rourke gave the major a perfunctory salute, if such a casual gesture could be called a salute. He said, "I'll go south, if it's all the same to you."

Moya grunted, "Then I'll go north." He was relieved because he knew most of the Cheyennes would be to the north.

He got out quickly, followed by Kiowa O'Rourke. On the gallery he stopped, withdrew his pipe and smoked it, afterward offering the tobacco pouch to O'Rourke. O'Rourke took it and reached for his own stubby pipe. He studied Joe while he packed and lighted it. At last he said, "It's a hard line to draw but you don't seem to have no trouble drawin' it."

Joe glanced irritably at him. "What's hard? I bedded squaws before this one. That don't make me brother to every damned redskin in her tribe. A job's a job, old man."

"Yeah. It is, ain't it?" O'Rourke turned and tramped disapprovingly toward the stables at the far end of the compound. Joe Moya followed more slowly. He stopped at the sutler's store to settle up and to pick up his saddlebags. By the time he had finished that, O'Rourke was riding up the middle of the parade ground toward the gate.

54

CHAPTER 5

A mile down the Platte from Fort Kettering, Moya encountered a wood-cutting detail. He heard their axes and saws long before he saw them. There were ten men in all, six cutting wood, four standing guard. He raised a hand as he rode past and the greeting was acknowledged somewhat suspiciously by the troopers. He smiled humourlessly but he reminded himself that suspicion would not help his cause. He must conduct himself in a way that would allay suspicion. He must make himself trusted, no matter how hard it was. If they did not trust him, he would fail.

Last night he should have stayed in the barracks instead of in a room at the sutler's store and he should have been a lot more agreeable with Major Burkhalter this morning. He should have been pleasant with O'Rourke. He should, at least, have acted the way Joe Moya, untroubled by grief and the hunger for vengeance, would have acted three days ago.

He selected a long, shallow draw leading out of the river-bed and followed it for several miles. If the Cheyennes weren't already watching Fort Kettering, they would be soon. He rode with a kind of indolent watchfulness, slouched and comfortable in his saddle, missing nothing either on the land or in the sky.

The massacre at Cut Nose Creek had changed many things for Joe Moya and he was aware of the change. Many Cheyennes knew him, but more did not. To most Cheyennes, even to some of those he knew, he was now simply a white man, an enemy. They would kill him on sight if they could. They would kill him as quickly as they would the ten troopers in the wood-cutting detail. Or as quickly as they would kill the paymaster and his escort after they had left the fort.

He travelled steadily all day. He knew this land, knew its creeks and its divides. As well as the Cheyennes, he knew where the deer were and where were the buffalo. He also knew where the Cheyenne villages were. Or at least he knew where they had been before the killing at Cut Nose Creek. And if they were no longer there, he knew the most likely places to look for them.

He made a large circle that day, a sixty-mile arc, and he found where three small villages had been. That night he camped in a shallow drainage known as Clearwater Creek. He built no fire. He gnawed on some cooked venison he had brought from the sutler's kitchen and drank water from the creek. As soon as it was dark, he picketed his horse and the packhorse and lay down to sleep, his rifle close at hand.

He did not sleep immediately, despite the fact that he was very tired. He kept seeing, in the darkness above him, or perhaps only in his mind, the face of Red Earth Woman. She had been only twenty-three. Little Squirrel had been six. Laughing Girl had been but four.

His eyes burned and tears overflowed and ran silently across his cheeks. The face of Red Earth Woman blurred and its place was taken by that of Little Squirrel, and later by that of Laughing Girl.

Suddenly he rolled onto his side, doubling as though a convulsion had taken him. His body shook, and the choked sounds of all but silent sobs came from him as though torn out by force. He was a strong man and death was commonplace to him. But his love had been great and the loss was almost impossible for him to bear.

How long would it be before her face stopped coming to him in the night? How long before he stopped remembering the petal softness of Laughing Girl's cheek against his own weathered one, or the way she would go into gales of delighted laughter

when his moustache tickled her? How long
before he stopped seeing the sturdy strength
of Little Squirrel walking along the village
street, his head thrown back, a toy bow
gripped firmly in his chubby hand?

He got up suddenly and began to pace
nervously back and forth. He paced, and
paced, until some of the agony had left his
thoughts, until he was weary and ready to
go to sleep. Then he lay down again.

He went to sleep, a light sleep that was
disturbed by each small noise. A hunting
owl, sweeping low after a mouse, rustled the
long grass and made him open his eyes,
made his hand touch the receiver of his gun.
A deer, browsing along the creek bottom,
also wakened him, as did one of his horses,
startled and made uneasy by a passing wolf.
Each time, after he had identified the
sound, he returned to sleep.

He was up half an hour before dawn,
before the faintest of grey lines streaked the
horizon in the east. Again he ate a small
amount of cooked venison and drank water
from the creek. He splashed water into his
face, stropped his razor, and shaved by feel.
He was in the saddle before he could see
objects fifty yards ahead and riding north
again.

At mid-morning he struck the drainage of

Cut Nose Creek several miles below the site of the massacre. Keeping to windward, he circled around the dead village, then entered the creek bottom upstream from it.

There was plenty of trail here had he been inclined to follow it. He did not because it wasn't necessary. He knew where the refugees were heading and he knew how dangerous it was to follow them. From here on he could be killed at any instant, by a gun he might not even hear. He also knew what must be done could be done in no other way.

Ten miles above the village ruins, he left the bed of the creek and headed up a long rise leading east. Now he rode openly, knowing he could not conceal himself. But he tried to stay on fairly level ground where there was no brush, where there were no arroyos where a bush-whacking Cheyenne could hide.

The village he sought lay in the drainage of Wolf Creek. He crossed over a low ridge and saw it near noon that second day, and without pausing, rode toward it down the slope.

He held the horses at a slow, deliberate walk. He saw the way the Cheyennes stopped what they were doing to stare at him. He saw the group of mounted braves

that left the village confines and rode galloping toward him. He paid them no heed.
He rode as though he belonged here, as
though he were one of them. But all the
time he knew it would take but one anxious
finger on the trigger of a single gun and he
would be dead, the village on Cut Nose
Creek unavenged.

They approached him, howling, and
passed him and pulled up their horses and
whirled around. He continued at the same
steady walk, but there was a spot in the
middle of his back that seemed to draw itself
together in anticipation of a bullet striking
it. He heard them coming at a gallop behind
him but he did not turn his head.

He reached the village edge. He had been
in this village before and knew where the
chief's tipi was. He rode directly to it, the
braves following silently now, confused and
uncertain as to what they should do. He
smiled grimly to himself as he swung from
the saddle.

The commotion brought Tall Elk from the
lodge. He stared at Joe Moya, no recogni-
tion changing the cold expression in his
eyes. Speaking in Cheyenne, Joe said, "I also
grieve for the dead ones on Cut Nose
Creek. Red Earth Woman is dead, and so is
Little Squirrel and so is Laughing Girl. I

buried them myself."

Still Tall Elk's expression did not change. Joe Moya said, "They are dead and cannot be brought back to life. But they can be avenged. I will avenge them, with your help or without."

A flicker of interest touched Tall Elk's eyes. Moya said, "I am one with the Cheyennes. I have lived and hunted with you for seven years. The Cheyennes will fight the pony soldiers of the whites. Even if I am dead, the Cheyennes will fight. But I can help. The pony soldiers do not know that I am more Cheyenne than white. They trust me to bring them information about the Cheyenne villages."

The interest in Tall Elk's eyes was stronger now. He turned and entered his lodge, and Moya followed him. Tall Elk seated himself at the fire in the centre of it. Moya went behind him and sat down too. One of Tall Elk's squaws brought his pipe. He packed it, pointed the stem at the four directions, at the earth and at the sky, then lighted it with a flaming twig from the fire. He puffed several times, then passed the pipe to Moya, who also puffed it solemnly before passing it back to the chief.

Moya knew the Cheyenne way would be to lead up to what was in his mind gradually but he was white enough to be impatient. He said, "The pony soldiers want a fight with the Cheyennes. They would like to fight another sleeping village like the one on Cut Nose Creek, so that they will not lose many men, so that the soldier chief will be made a bigger soldier chief by the father in Washington."

Tall Elk nodded without speaking.

Moya went on. "Let us give them a sleeping village then, Tall Elk. Let us give them what looks like a sleeping village but one that is wide awake, with five warriors in every lodge. Then, when they attack, let us bring mounted warriors from behind to slaughter them."

Tall Elk's eyes gleamed with open interest now. He asked, "And where would this village be?"

Moya said, "Not here. This is too close to Cut Nose Creek and the pony soldiers will be suspicious, expecting an ambush here. It should be at some place far away." He had been thinking of a possible location for the planned ambush. It had to be a place where there was concealment behind the village for several hundred mounted Cheyennes. One such place was on Rialto Creek, seventy-five miles west. He said, "Do you know the place the white men call Rialto

Creek?"

Tall Elk nodded. Moya went on to describe the exact spot he had in mind, and Tall Elk nodded vigorously.

Moya said, "Set up a village there. It will be five days before I get back to the fort, at least seven before they will be able to attack. It will be seven days, but it may be more. You must make the village look as any village might. If they are suspicious they will not attack, but will run away."

Tall Elk studied him carefully. Moya could see that Tall Elk did not trust him. He could also see that the chief was thinking nothing could go wrong. His scouts would tell him before the attack how many pony soldiers there were. He would have them outnumbered. Moya could not betray him. He nodded finally, got to his feet, and stepped outside. Moya followed him.

The young mounted warriors still sat their fidgeting ponies, waiting for him to reappear. Tall Elk said, "Let him go in peace. He is one of us."

Sullenly they stared at Moya, as sullenly stared down at their chief. Moya mounted his horse. He said, "Seven days, Tall Elk. The village must be there in seven days."

"It will be there as you say."

Moya nodded, reined his horse around,

and, still leading the packhorse, rode away, frowning to himself. He did not underrate the risks he had taken coming here. Yet something bothered him. It had been too easy. He suddenly wondered if the village would indeed be there on Rialto Creek seven days from now. Perhaps Tall Elk intended to have him murdered on the way back to Fort Kettering.

He cleared the edge of the village and rode up the slope toward the southwest, where Fort Kettering was. Behind him was silence, silence that suddenly seemed ominous. With difficulty, he resisted the almost irresistible compulsion to look around.

He travelled slowly now, killing time, not wanting to arrive back at Fort Kettering much before the seven days were up. He camped, and sometimes he hunted, but always he stayed alert. Other bands would not know of his arrangement with Tall Elk. They would kill him on sight.

And in the evenings, when the shadows lengthened and the sunlight on the land was gold, he thought of Red Earth Woman, and smelled her clean woman-smell as he embraced her, and he heard the children yelling at their play. And the agonizing ache of loss came back and twisted his face and made his eyes grow hard.

On the evening of the seventh day he came to the gate at Fort Kettering and called to the trooper on the tower platform, "Open up, trooper. It's Joe Moya to see Major Burkhalter."

The gate swung open and Joe rode in, trailing his packhorse behind. The gate closed behind him. Joe had not missed the fact, riding in, that the wood detail was no longer cutting wood. He rode down the middle of the parade, looking neither to right nor left. He dismounted at the stables, led his horses in, and unsaddled them. He put them in stalls and left his saddle and pack-saddle in the tack room, removing only his saddlebags. With them slung over a shoulder, he walked out onto the parade.

The sun was already down. The smell of cooking food was in the air. Joe stopped at the sutler's store and got a handful of cigars. Then he walked up the gallery toward headquarters. Twice he spoke to a trooper that he knew.

Idly he wondered what O'Rourke had found to the south of here. Nothing, he hoped, that would sound more inviting to the major than the village on Rialto Creek.

Burkhalter was waiting for him, having seen him ride into the fort. Joe was directed into his office immediately. He offered the major a cigar and waited while Burkhalter lighted it. Then he said, "Villages are on the move, Major, for a radius of fifty miles. You scared the pants off 'em."

"What do you mean, on the move? Heading where?"

Joe grinned mirthlessly. "Away from Fort Kettering. They're puttin' distance between them an' you. Isn't that what O'Rourke said?"

"He isn't back yet."

Joe felt himself relax with relief. He said, "I found one village, Major, that I figure might stay put. It's about forty miles from here — on Rialto Creek."

Burkhalter reached for a map, unrolled it and spread it out. Joe got up and went to his side. He pointed to Rialto Creek, tracing it from its source to the place where he had told Tall Elk the village ought to be. He jabbed a strong, stubby finger at the spot and the major marked it with a cross. Joe said, "Medium-sized village, Major, about the size of that one on Cut Nose Creek. I didn't dare get in too close because it's open season on everybody with a white skin but I got in close enough. I'd say sixty warriors at the most, but it might be smart to figure eighty just in case."

Burkhalter nodded. There was a new,

bright gleam about his eyes. His mouth had a strange set to it. Joe thought with angry savagery, "It ain't just promotion he wants. He likes the killin' too."

He got up, put his back to the major, and walked to the window. He stared out, fighting for self-control. More than he had ever wanted anything, he wanted to bury his knife in the major's straining paunch. He said, "Major, I'd like to get cleaned up and eat. Is there anything else you want right now?"

"No, Mr. Moya. No. You go ahead."

Moya stepped toward the door, avoiding Burkhalter's eyes.

Burkhalter said, "Good job, Moya. Good job."

Moya turned his head, hoping the frantic hatred he was feeling wouldn't show. But the major wasn't even looking at him. He was staring at the map spread out on his desk.

Joe Moya opened the door and went out. He nodded curtly at the corporal on duty and crossed to the outside door. He stepped out onto the gallery, suddenly puffing furiously on his cigar.

He threw it from him violently and it made a shower of sparks to show where it had struck.

Clenching his jaws — with fists doubled — Joe Moya walked toward the sutler's store. Right now he wanted a drink more than he wanted food. He needed something to get the bitter taste out of his mouth, to calm the raging anger in his mind.

CHAPTER 6

For a long time after the scout had left, Burkhalter stared down at the map spread out on his desk and at the cross marking the village on Rialto Creek. He picked up a pencil and thoughtfully marked a second cross on Cut Nose Creek, where the Cheyenne village had been.

Immediately after his return from that engagement he had sent a report of it to Departmental Headquarters at Omaha. As was usually the case, the telegraph wires had been down and he had been forced to send the message by courier to Fort Laramie, from which point it had been telegraphed to Omaha. Now he crossed the room and opened the door leading to the outer office. Corporal Ord was on duty. Burkhalter said, "See if the wires are still down, Corporal. If not, let me know. I want to send a telegram."

Ord got up, saluted, and went out.

Burkhalter returned to his office, leaving the door ajar. He sat down at his desk and swiftly wrote the message out, addressing it to General Stiles, Headquarters, Dept. of the Platte, Omaha. It read: "Have located band of hostiles camped on Rialto Creek, raiding ranches and killing settlers. Request permission to attack and rescue white captives believed taken on recent raids." He signed the message, "Samuel Burkhalter, Commandant, Fort Kettering," and scrawled "Urgent" across the face of it.

Ord returned. "The line's been repaired, Major. You can get a message through." He grinned slightly and added, "As long as no buffalo bull rubs against a pole before I get back there with it."

Burkhalter handed him the message. "Have the telegrapher on duty send this one, then. And tell him to wait for a reply."

"Yes, sir." Ord took the message and, without looking at it, hurried out.

Burkhalter began to pace nervously back and forth. The message he had just handed Corporal Ord was not really intended to request permission for anything. It would serve another purpose, a more important one. It would bring him forcefully to the attention of his superiors and since it dealt with making war when the plains were supposed to be at peace, consideration of it involved governmental policy and would, therefore, also bring his proposed action to the attention of the War Department and, perhaps, even to that of the President.

This was precisely what he wanted, but waiting made him nervous. He hoped the telegraph line wouldn't stay intact very long and doubted if it would, particularly with the Cheyennes stirred up. He didn't want to be in too close contact with headquarters in the coming days. He wanted to feel free to act as he saw fit. He knew from past experience that once an action is taken — if it is successful — it is usually approved. And he meant to see that the action on Rialto Creek would be as successful as the one on Cut Nose Creek had been. But suppose his request for permission was denied? What would he do then?

His jaw clenched angrily. Hell, he'd attack anyway. General Stiles knew as well as he how hard it was to get Indians to stand and fight. A man had to catch them where he could.

Ord did not return. The major continued to pace back and forth, scowling and chewing on the dead stub of his cigar. Ord had, he supposed, stopped at the sutler's store for a cup of coffee and a bite to eat.

An hour passed. At last, Burkhalter heard Ord's footsteps hurrying along the gallery. The corporal came in.

"Two messages, Major," he said and handed them to Burkhalter. He retired immediately and closed the door.

The first message was blunt and to the point.

"Maj. Samuel Burkhalter, Commandant, Fort Kettering. Request denied." It was signed, "Wilson Stiles, Commanding General, Dept. of the Platte, Omaha."

Scowling angrily, Burkhalter read the second telegram. It was also signed by the general and said: "Parents of Private Isaac Shore, killed in action Cut Nose Creek, en route Fort Kettering under escort to view his grave. Extend every consideration."

Burkhalter's scowl deepened and he cursed savagely beneath his breath. That was all he needed — a couple of grieving civilians that had to be entertained and shown around.

But that wasn't the worst of it. He could detail one of his junior officers to entertain Mr. and Mrs. Shore. What really bothered him was the first telegram, and those blunt, uncompromising words, "Request denied."

Well to hell with the general. He'd go ahead anyway. He heard steps on the gal-

71

lery and heard the outside door open again. A few moments later Corporal Ord knocked and came in with yet another telegram. He said, "Line's down now, Major. It went dead right in the middle of this one."

Burkhalter took the message from him. It read, in crisp, impersonal words: "Forward evidence of Cheyenne depredations taken at Cut Nose Creek for examination immediately under escort ten troo . . ." The message ended there.

Burkhalter wadded it up angrily and threw it across the room. Damn them, did they doubt his word? Did they doubt that the Cheyennes were raiding and taking scalps?

He sat down nervously at his desk. The telegraph line was down now, at least. They couldn't send him any more orders from Omaha, at least orders that would reach him before he left to attack the village on Rialto Creek.

His angry colour began to fade. A slight smile touched his mouth. Maybe those scalps taken at Cut Nose Creek weren't fresh enough to prove recent depredations against the whites. Perhaps the articles belonging to whites weren't conclusive and could have been traded for legitimately. But he was willing to bet that things would be different on Rialto Creek. There'd be fresh scalps there, taken from white settlers since the affair at Cut Nose Creek. And who would know, in Omaha, whether they came from a village on Rialto Creek or from one on Cut Nose Creek?

He leaned back in his swivel chair. He lighted a fresh cigar and puffed furiously on it.

At eight, Lieutenant Martin Keefe left his room. He stood on the gallery long enough to take a cigar from his tunic pocket, bite off the end, and light it up. Puffing contentedly, he crossed the parade to the north wall.

The moon had not yet risen and the sky was thinly overcast and very black. Lights glowed in the windows across the dark parade. A match flared at the gate as a sentry lighted up his pipe. Someone was yelling down in the barracks. A dog barked. A guitar made a softly plaintive music that was nearly drowned out by other noise.

A door opened across the parade. Silhouetted against the light inside, Keefe saw Martha Burkhalter step out onto the gallery. The door closed and darkness swallowed her.

He leaned back against the wall, staring at the windows of headquarters where he knew the major was to-night.

He wondered what Burkhalter would do in the days to come. He had sent both Moya and O'Rourke out to scout, which meant he was looking for Cheyenne villages to attack. Moya was back but Keefe had not yet heard what his report had been. Moya had probably found one or more Cheyenne villages and preparations for an expedition against them would begin immediately. Within a week they would undoubtedly see action against the Indians.

He heard the murmur of voices from the direction of the gate, and a moment later heard it squeak. Uneasily he walked that way, connecting Mrs. Burkhalter's appearance on the gallery instantly with the opening of the gate. Surely she wouldn't be foolish enough to go outside the fort. Not now. And not at night.

The trooper on duty at the gate saluted him. Keefe asked immediately, "Who just went out?"

"Mrs. Burkhalter, sir. She often goes out for a walk at night."

Keefe uttered a low-voiced curse. He said, "Open the gate, trooper. And from now on, nobody goes out at night — not without the approval of the officer of the day. Is that clear?"

"Yes, sir." The trooper sounded scared.

He swung the gate open enough for Keefe to squeeze through. Keefe called back, "Close it, trooper. I'll let you know when I get back."

The gate squeaked closed. He stared into the blackness ahead of him. The road made a pale path toward the river bluff. He thought he saw a darker patch in the middle of the road. . . .

He broke into a trot, not wanting to call out, not wanting to alert any Cheyennes that might be skulking about. Probably, he thought, the nearest Indian was miles away. But a man could not be sure. . . .

He was half-way to the black figure now and he could make it out a little in spite of the lack of light. It was a woman's figure that stopped, and turned . . .

Keefe heard, and she apparently heard at the same time he did. The pound of a horse's rapidly running hooves, drawing close, coming swiftly on. . . .

Keefe was still fifty feet away from her, now running hard. The woman stopped and Keefe yelled, "Get down on the ground — or run! Don't just stand there and wait!" He felt a raging helplessness and a furious anger at her stupidity. She should know it was dangerous to go outside the fort at night, particularly since the massacre of the village on Cut Nose Creek. The Cheyennes would like nothing better than to capture the commandant's wife.

A hard-ridden horse appeared from his right, running toward the road, heading directly toward the wife of the commandant. Martha Burkhalter stood frozen in the centre of the road. Suddenly she turned and tried to escape.

The horseman swept past her, missing his grab for her because of the sudden way she moved. He yanked his horse to a rearing, turning halt. Martha Burkhalter tried to dodge, tried to run again. Keefe bawled, "Drop to the ground! Force him to get off his horse!"

But she either was not thinking, or did not hear. From a dozen feet away Keefe caught a glimpse of her face, white with terror now.

No time to seize her and carry her to safety. No time for anything. He hit her with his shoulder, knocking her full twenty feet into the brush at the side of the road. She uttered a terror-stricken sound that was half cry of pain, half gasp of surprise. Her body crashed into the brush and was still.

Keefe grabbed for his service revolver, remembered that it was hanging on the chair-back in his room. He was weaponless against a Cheyenne brave mounted and armed and hungry for vengeance . . .

He smelled the sweaty reek of the Indian's horse. The animal's shoulder struck him, knocking him to his knees, perhaps saving him from having his skull split open by the steel tomahawk. Again the Indian yanked the horse into a rearing turn. His rifle was now in his hands instead of the tomahawk.

Flame belched from the muzzle of the gun. Keefe rolled frantically across the road as bullets dug into the ground beside him, showering him with dirt.

He reached the side of the road, the concealment and protection of the brush. Still silent, the Indian leaped from his horse's back and ran toward him like a cat.

Keefe froze. He was thoroughly scared. Hand-to-hand combat with a well-armed Cheyenne was more than he had bargained for. He wondered what was taking the men inside the fort so long, then realised fleetingly that this whole business probably hadn't taken more than a minute or two.

Martha Burkhalter chose this instant to scream. The sound was a shrill cry of utter terror that made a chill run down Keefe's spine. But it turned the Indian aside. Half a dozen feet from him, the Indian veered away toward the sound of the scream.

Keefe got to his feet and dived, arms outstretched. He caught the Indian's legs with his hands and brought the brave crashing to the ground.

He scrambled toward the man. The Indian's rifle swung and the barrel slammed against Keefe's shoulder, instantly turning it numb. Martha Burkhalter screamed again.

Then there was the sound of the squeaking gates, and the shouts of men, and the pound of many running feet.

Again the rifle barrel slammed against Lieutenant Keefe. This time he lost his hold.

The Indian sprang nimbly to his feet. He disappeared like a ghost into the brush. For several moments, Keefe could hear him crashing down the river bluff.

He struggled to his feet. He staggered toward the direction from which he had heard the scream. The Indian's horse spooked from him and also disappeared over the edge of the bluff.

He saw her rise, saw her run toward him. Then she was in his arms, sobbing, trembling violently as if she had a chill. Again he smelled her light fragrance and felt the silkiness of her hair tickling his nose. He felt the warmth, the fullness of her body as it pressed so tightly against his own.

His hands gripped her arms. He held her

forcibly away. Good God, if the major saw them this way . . .

He heard Burkhalter's harsh voice. "What the hell's going on out here! What the hell are you doing outside the gates?"

Martha Burkhalter's trembling abruptly stopped. She turned rigid in Keefe's grasp. He released her and she stumbled toward the major, who folded her in his arms.

Captain MacPhee was at Keefe's side. They were surrounded by troopers carrying guns. MacPhee said, "What happened, Keefe?"

"I heard the major's wife go out the gate. I knew it was dangerous and followed her to bring her back. The Indian tried to grab her but he didn't make it stick. I guess that's all."

MacPhee yelled, "Back in the fort, you men! The Indian's gone!"

The men straggled back into the fort, following the major and his now-weeping wife. MacPhee and Keefe brought up the rear. When they reached the gate, MacPhee turned to Keefe. "See the surgeon, Keefe. Let him take a look at you."

Keefe nodded. He waited until Burkhalter and his wife had disappeared into their quarters. Then he headed for the post hospital. He wished he could forget the way

Martha Burkhalter had pressed herself against him out there. He wished he could forget the way she had smelled, her warmth, the soft fullness of her body . . .

But he could not forget. She had been in his thoughts since his arrival here, and that, he suspected, was the way she wanted it. But he had better get her out of his thoughts and keep her out. She was Major Burkhalter's wife. That one fact was unchangeable.

CHAPTER 7

Keefe walked rather painfully along the parade to the post hospital. All around him, troopers were discussing the incident excitedly. Keefe heard one say, "Them sons-a-bitches sure learn hard. Looks like we'll have to kick the hell out of them again."

Another breathed, "Good God, if he'd a got the major's wife away from here . . . You know what Injuns do to a white woman?"

"No, what?"

"They stake her out, that's what, an' they all use her until they're through with her. If she's still alive an' able to travel, they take her back an' make a slave out of her."

Keefe didn't know whether the trooper knew what he was talking about or not but apparently the others believed he did.

80

A week ago, he thought, this country had been peaceful. Now it was at war. Burkhalter must know that isolated settlers would pay with their lives and property for what he had done at Cut Nose Creek but apparently he didn't care. Already he was planning something else, something that would make the whole thing worse.

Keefe reached the post hospital and went inside. Dr. Lynch came in a moment later. "MacPhee says you tangled with an Indian outside the gate. Where are you hurt?"

"I don't think I am. He hit my shoulder with his rifle and it's pretty sore but I think I'll live all right."

"Take off your tunic and let's have a look at it."

Keefe unbuttoned his dusty tunic and slipped it off. His shirt followed it. He unbuttoned his underwear and struggled out of the upper half. He glanced down at the shoulder. There was already a bruise on it as big as the palm of his hand, an ugly reddish blue. Lynch whistled. "Bet that's sore. And it'll be worse in the morning. I'll rub it with some liniment. Sit down over there."

Keefe sat down. He caught himself thinking again of Martha Burkhalter, remembering how she had felt in his arms. He felt his

81

face heating and hoped the surgeon didn't notice it.

Lynch got a bottle of liniment, poured some into his palm, and began to rub the bruise and the surrounding area. "Liniment won't help that bruise but it'll help the sore muscles some."

Keefe sat patiently, waiting for the surgeon to finish. When he had, he got to his feet, shrugged into his underwear top, and put his shirt and tunic on. The liniment was a strong but not unpleasant smell. Dr. Lynch said, "It'll be stiff in the morning, Keefe. Come in then and I'll rub it with liniment again."

"Thank you."

"Mrs. Burkhalter is an attractive woman, isn't she?"

Keefe glanced sharply up but the surgeon wasn't looking at him. Keefe said, "She is. Yes, sir."

"And young for the major too."

Keefe frowned. "What are you trying to say to me, sir?"

Lynch looked up and met his glance. "She is the major's wife, Lieutenant Keefe."

Keefe felt his face burning. It angered him and he said intemperately, "Doctor, I am not likely to forget. I do not need you reminding me."

"Of course not, Keefe. I'm sorry. I guess I was out of line." The surgeon seemed genuinely contrite. Keefe grinned thinly.

But as he walked along the gallery toward his quarters, he was not sure he did not need reminding that Martha was Burkhalter's wife. And he also knew he would lie awake for a long time to-night remembering how warm and full her body had been and how eagerly she had pressed herself close to him. It could have been terror and relief at being rescued, of course. It could have been sudden release from that moment of intolerable strain. Or it could have been deliberate. He was the newest man on the post.

As he passed headquarters, he glanced in the open door. Burkhalter and Joe Moya were in Burkhalter's office, bent over the desk, studying a map. He went on, angry at himself for the way tension kept building in him as he approached the Burkhalters' door.

He reached it, saw that it was open, and knew she was waiting for him. He heard her softly say, "Lieutenant."

He halted and glanced in at her. She was standing in the middle of the room. The lamplight was behind her, throwing her face into shadow but silhouetting the full, womanly curves of her body. She said, "Come in a moment, Lieutenant."

He stepped into the room. He was almost thirty and there had been a number of women in his life. But none that had stirred him the way this one did. None that made him hunger as violently as this. It was a raw thing, an elemental thing he had never experienced before. The fact that she was the major's wife seemed not important — not important at all.

She said softly, "I want to thank you, Lieutenant Keefe. For coming out after me. When I think of what would be happening to me right now . . ."

He could visualise it in his mind and suddenly understood that was exactly what she wanted him to do. She was playing with him, sure of him. He couldn't help wanting her but he could be and was suddenly angry at her for being so goddamned sure. He said, his voice deliberate and cold, "Thanks is not necessary, Mrs. Burkhalter. I would have done the same thing for the post laundress that I did for you." He backed toward the door.

He thought she would cross the room and strike him but she did not. He turned and strode toward his quarters, waiting for the door to slam behind him.

It did, resoundingly. He reached his own

door, opened it, and went inside. He lighted the lamp and with hands that trembled violently, lowered the chimney and trimmed the wick. He sat down on the edge of the bed and released a long sigh of pent-up breath.

He had never met a woman like Martha Burkhalter. Never had he encountered a woman capable of stirring such violence in him. He felt like a man standing at the edge of an abyss, knowing that to sway only slightly toward it would be to fall and be lost.

If he ever took her, if he ever let himself . . . There would be no hope for him. Having had her once, he would do anything to have her again, and again and again after that.

He grinned uneasily to himself, wondering from what recess of his mind had come the deliberate words he had said to her, when the words he had been thinking, the words he had wanted to say, had been quite different. Perhaps, he thought, it was a deeply buried instinct of self-preservation that made a man do one thing while every thought is screaming at him to do another.

He heard a step outside his door and a moment later heard a knock. He crossed to the door and opened it, half afraid he would see Martha Burkhalter standing there. But it was Captain MacPhee, a slight grin on his face, a bottle and two glasses in his hand. He said, "The surgeon says you got quite a lick. I thought perhaps a little snort would help you sleep."

Keefe stood aside and let MacPhee come in, wondering as he did if MacPhee had seen him step into Burkhalter's quarters earlier.

MacPhee crossed the room, put bottle and glasses down on the commode, and pulled the cork. Keefe closed the door. MacPhee said, "Say when."

Keefe waited until the glass was half full before he spoke and afterward felt MacPhee's penetrating glance on him. MacPhee poured a drink for himself, then brought the first one to Keefe. He touched his glass to Keefe's and said, "Cheers, Lieutenant Keefe."

Keefe took a gulp of the stuff and looked at MacPhee gratefully. MacPhee sat down on the edge of the bed and sipped his drink. "I take it you're not married, Keefe. Ever come close?"

"Once or twice." There was suddenly a companionable kind of closeness between the two despite the difference in rank and age. MacPhee said, "I've been married once, almost twice. Women are strange and headstrong creatures, Keefe, or at least I have found them so, for ever needing proof that men find them desirable."

Keefe said dryly, "You are talking about Martha Burkhalter, I think."

MacPhee glanced at him with startled surprise. Suddenly a grin began to grow on his face and an instant later he was chuckling wholeheartedly. "I didn't know I was so obvious. I guess it is just that each new officer needs to be warned. The man you replaced would not listen and nearly got himself called out for his pains."

"Burkhalter knows how she is?"

MacPhee nodded. "He knows, Keefe. He knows." MacPhee finished his drink, got up, and crossed the room. He poured another, turned, and looked at Keefe. "I saw her call you in a few moments ago. It is well-meant advice that I give you, Keefe. She's a beautiful woman and she knows how to stir a man."

Keefe did not reply.

MacPhee finished his drink and put down the glass. "I'll leave the bottle, Keefe, in case you want another one."

Keefe thanked him. He closed the door behind MacPhee and listened to his retreating footsteps on the gallery. He began to pace back and forth, scowling at first, smiling at last. The officers on this post were like a brood of mother hens, he thought wryly to himself, and he seemed to be their chick. Yet he was grateful too and he could understand their concern. There can be nothing more explosive on a lonely frontier post than a woman like Martha Burkhalter, particularly when she is married to the commanding officer. Burkhalter's subordinates must be walking a tight wire all the time trying to keep things from blowing up.

He found himself actually looking forward to the coming campaign against the Cheyennes. At least he would be off the post and away from her. He would have time to regain his equilibrium and to get things back into proper perspective in his mind. His words a while ago had made her violently angry at him. But he was not at all sure her anger would endure.

CHAPTER 8

It was Joe Moya who spotted the parents of Private Shore, approaching from the east with an eight man escort. He had been on the wall looking for Kiowa O'Rourke, who had not returned and was now overdue. He called to the trooper below on the ground and the man shouted for the corporal of the guard, afterward opening the gates.

Burkhalter came out onto the gallery in front of headquarters and watched the Shores' light spring wagon rattle into the fort. Captain Leighton, who was officer of the day, came out at Burkhalter's summons. The major said, "Get Lieutenant Keefe. Detail him to talk to the Shores and to show them around."

Leighton said, "Yes, sir." He walked briskly along the gallery to the post hospital, where he knew Keefe was. Keefe was sitting beside Lieutenant Hargreaves's bed. They were both smoking cigars and grinning at something one of them had said. Keefe rose as Captain Leighton came in. The captain said, "Major Burkhalter wants you to talk to the Shores and to show them around. They've just arrived. Put 'em in the quarters next to mine."

Keefe nodded, glanced at Hargreaves, and said, "See you again, Lieutenant." He stepped out onto the gallery, squinting against the bright rays of the sun.

The spring wagon and escort had halted in front of headquarters. The corporal of the guard was standing there talking to the driver of the wagon. Mr. and Mrs. Shore had alighted and stood beside the wagon looking around in bewilderment.

Keefe hurried along the gallery toward them. When he reached them he removed his hat and extended his hand to Mr. Shore. "I'm Lieutenant Keefe. I have been asked to show you around." He glanced at the corporal. "Have their luggage brought to the quarters next to Captain Leighton's, Corporal."

"Yes, sir."

Shore was a stocky, middle-aged man, grey of hair, wearing a short, trimmed beard. He was dressed in a business suit that was now wrinkled and dusty from the trip. He wore gold-rimmed glasses with thick lenses that seemed to magnify his eyes. He peered at Keefe. "Did you know our boy?"

Keefe shook his head as he led them toward the quarters that had been assigned to them. "I'm sorry, sir. I just arrived here at Fort Kettering."

"We would like to know how he was killed."

Keefe stared at the man with mild dismay, then switched his glance to Mrs. Shore. She was a slight, sweet-faced woman, who was now wearing a timid, hesitant smile. Keefe said, "He was killed in action against the Indians, sir, at Cut Nose Creek. Would you like to rest a little while or do you want to see his grave now?"

Mr. Shore glanced at his wife and she nodded slightly. He returned his glance to Keefe. "We would like to see his grave now, Lieutenant, if that is all right with you."

"Of course." Keefe stopped and glanced back at the wagon. He said, "Wait here a moment, please." He left them and hurried back to the wagon in time to stop the mounted troopers who had escorted it. "I want four of you to follow me and Mr. and Mrs. Shore to the cemetery outside the gate."

A sergeant saluted him and called off three names. He and the three whose names he had called dismounted and followed Keefe, leading their horses. Keefe returned to the Shores. "The cemetery is outside the gate. If you will come with me . . ."

He led the way across the sun-washed parade to the gate, which the sentry opened for them. He went out, followed by the Shores and by the four-man escort, mounted now.

From the front gate of the fort the land stretched away across the Platte for what looked like a thousand miles. Shore stopped and stared at the view for a moment. The air was clear and the smell of sage was strong. Shore said, "This is a beautiful land, Lieutenant, but it is a terrible land as well."

Keefe didn't know what to say. Private Shore had been the only casualty in the battle of Cut Nose Creek, except for Lieutenant Hargreaves, who would recover completely. Yet he understood that to Mr. and Mrs. Shore the loss was enormous. Private Shore had been their only son.

Mrs. Shore said softly, "You are making the Lieutenant feel badly, Nathan."

Shore said immediately, "I am sorry, Lieutenant. It is just hard for me to believe that he is gone."

Keefe said, "The cemetery is on the south wall, Mr. Shore. If you will follow me . . ." He rounded the corner and headed through the sagebrush toward the cemetery.

It was a bare-ground burial place, with white crosses laid out in exact lines. Private Shore's grave was easy to spot. The cross was whiter than the others were. The mound of earth had not yet settled from time and weather. There were no flowers on the grave.

Keefe lagged, allowing the bereaved couple to approach the grave alone. He turned his head and cautioned the four mounted men, "Look sharp. You're not out here for the ride."

Shore and his wife walked slowly, almost

hesitantly, to their son's final resting place. For a moment they stood forlornly at the foot of it, staring at the white cross marker at its head. Suddenly Mrs. Shore fell to her knees. Faintly Keefe heard her voice, "Our Father who art in heaven, hallowed be Thy name. Thy kingdom come, Thy will be done, on earth as it is in heaven. Give us this day . . ." He felt tears burning behind his eyes and blinked rapidly. For a moment he was angry, wishing Major Burkhalter had assumed this task. He should have to witness the simple grief of these two people, because he was the cause of it. His ambition had killed Private Shore just as surely as it had killed fifty or sixty Indians. Nor was that the worst. The survivors of those murdered Indians were probably exacting their own vengeance even now against isolated settlers somewhere in this sparsely settled land. There were more battles to come, with more killing, more vengeance afterward. It was a circle, ever widening, like concentric circles spreading outward from a disturbance on the surface of a pond.

Mrs. Shore finished her prayer and now he could hear her weeping softly. He waited patiently. Her husband helped her to her feet. He stood there, arm around her shoulders, comforting her in a soft, deep voice.

The two turned and came toward Keefe, both trying to smile and put him at ease, neither succeeding very well. He said, "You may come out here again. At any time. Just be sure that you have an escort when you do."

He accompanied them back into the fort, and, once they were inside, dismissed the four-man detail that had escorted them. He led them across the parade to the quarters they had been assigned.

They thanked him and he withdrew. Their door closed. He headed for the officers' mess, wanting to talk to somebody, suddenly just wanting company.

Leighton and MacPhee were there ahead of him, and seemed to be arguing. He heard MacPhee say, ". . . and permission was refused. But he's going ahead with it anyway. He's planning to attack that village on Rialto Creek."

Leighton asked dryly, "What would you suggest we do? He's the commanding officer."

"I know that and I know how damned helpless we are. He is well regarded in some quarters in Washington. He held brevet brigadier rank during the war. If we oppose him . . ." MacPhee suddenly became aware of Keefe and stopped in mid-sentence almost guiltily. Leighton asked, "Did you get the Shores settled all right, Keefe?"

"I took them outside the wall to see the grave. I left them in their quarters afterward. I felt sorry for them. Private Shore was their only son."

MacPhee said, "Yes. It's too bad."

There was an awkward silence then, and at last Keefe blurted, "Can he get away with disobeying a direct order from the general?"

Both men looked embarrassed and he knew they wanted to avoid the subject — at least neither wanted to discuss it with him. But MacPhee replied, "He can and it appears he will. And who is to say whether he is wrong or not? The truce out here has admittedly been an uneasy one. Trouble was certain to come eventually. Both the Sioux and the Cheyenne are very arrogant and perhaps it is better that we choose the time and place that we shall fight."

Keefe didn't think MacPhee believed that philosophy, but he didn't say anything. Leighton drained his coffee cup and said, "I'd better get back to headquarters. Major Burkhalter is expecting Kiowa O'Rourke to return at any time. He is already overdue."

MacPhee, plainly relieved that the subject had been changed, asked, "Do you think something has happened to him?"

Leighton shrugged. "He was to have been back in a week. There has to be some explanation for the delay."

"What do you think of Moya?"

Leighton grinned. "I like O'Rourke better but I'll be damned if I can say why. Moya's a good tracker and he certainly understands the Indians."

Leighton left. Keefe got himself a cup of coffee. When he returned, Captain MacPhee asked, "What do you think of the Shores?"

Keefe smiled. "They're nice people. I liked them."

"Not the kind to make trouble?"

"I don't think so. Still, people like the Shores sometimes turn out to be surprisingly strong when they believe themselves to be fighting an injustice or a wrong."

MacPhee peered closely at him. "Wrong? What is wrong? This is a frontier army post charged with keeping the peace over thousands of square miles of empty land."

"You do not believe an unprovoked attack upon a sleeping village is a wrong?"

MacPhee glanced at the door. "I wouldn't advise you to let the major hear you saying that." His eyes were cold. "I wouldn't even advise you to think it. Not if you value your career."

"Sorry."

MacPhee smiled faintly, finished his coffee, and went out. Keefe sipped his thoughtfully. What Burkhalter had done at Cut Nose Creek *was* wrong. What he was planning to do to the village on Rialto Creek was just as wrong. Nevertheless Keefe knew that, in history books, Burkhalter could easily come out right. Even in the judgment of his superiors he would probably end up right, particularly if he succeeded in wiping the village out and if his own casualties were light.

He finished his coffee and went to the door. He was surprised to see Nathan Shore crossing the parade toward the barracks against the south wall. Shore stopped beside several troopers lounging in the sun. He conversed with them. Probably asking if they had known his son, thought Keefe.

He watched idly. Shore left the group and moved to another one. He stopped and talked to them similarly, then moved on again.

A bugler sounded officers call and Keefe walked toward headquarters. Burkhalter called him into his office. Leighton and MacPhee were already there. Mills and DuBois came in shortly afterward.

Burkhalter stared across the map-laden desk at them. "As you probably know, the scout Moya has brought in word that there is a village of hostiles on Rialto Creek. We will move out day after to-morrow and reach them at dawn of the second day following."

Nobody spoke. Burkhalter jabbed at a spot on one of the maps with a stubby forefinger. "There is a low bluff behind the village, and beyond that some rough country. I will take K Troop and part of B and attack from the bluff. Captain MacPhee will take L up the creek bottom and attack them from the lower side. The remainder of B Troop will remain here at the fort. Any questions?"

"How large is the village, sir?" This was MacPhee.

"Moya says sixty to eighty braves."

"Can we reach there without being observed?"

Burkhalter looked wryly at him. "We can try, MacPhee. We will leave here two hours before dawn. Moya will scout our back trail to determine if we have been observed, with orders to eliminate any Cheyenne scouts that he may find."

"Where's O'Rourke, Major? Do you have any idea?"

"O'Rourke is probably dead, Captain MacPhee. He would have returned by now if he was not."

Burkhalter stared speculatively at Keefe, a brooding something behind his eyes that was puzzling. Keefe followed the others out. Shore was still talking to the troopers on the other side of the parade.

Martha Burkhalter was standing on the gallery in front of her open door. He could feel her eyes on him. Made uneasy, he turned the other way. Behind him he heard Burkhalter talking as the major came out onto the gallery with Leighton and MacPhee. Burkhalter's voice stopped suddenly in mid-sentence but after a moment went on again.

Keefe headed for the stables irritably.

CHAPTER 9

If anybody noticed Joe Moya's apparent concern over O'Rourke's failure to return, nobody mentioned it. But he was concerned, and obviously so. Except for meals and for a minimum of sleep, and except for an occasional short scout in the immediate vicinity of the fort, he spent all his time in the tower at the northeast corner of the fort.

Even when he was asleep, in one of the bachelor officer's rooms, he was alert, waking at each change of sentries, waking each time one of them called out. He wanted to be first to talk to Kiowa O'Rourke. He wanted to be first to know what Kiowa had found and what his report to Major Burkhalter was going to be.

On the ninth night, Kiowa finally returned. Afoot he came, having lost his horse, and Joe Moya saw him first from the tower beside the gate. He called softly down to the sentry and the gate squeaked open. O'Rourke came through, to find Moya waiting for him in the soft darkness of the bare parade. He looked at Moya, unable to see his face clearly, and grunted softly, "When the hell did you get back?"

"Couple days ago. Looks like you had some trouble, Irish."

"Some. Got jumped by a scouting party last night and had to leave my horse. I don't take to walkin' much."

"What'd you find?"

"The Svenson ranch burned out — Svenson's daughters laying there naked in the sun. I buried 'em. I found old man Brandywine burnt to death in his shack." He fished for his pipe. Moya handed him a cigar, took one for himself, and held a match cupped until both were lighted. "Find any villages?" he asked.

O'Rourke puffed for several moments on

his cigar without answering. He said softly, "It's good to be back. It's good to loosen up an' know I ain't goin' to git a scalpin' knife in the back."

Moya repeated, "Find any villages?"

O'Rourke peered at him. "Nary a one that was stayin' still. I found a couple trails of movin' ones, but nothin' the major could rightly hit."

Moya felt a touch of deep relief.

O'Rourke went on, "Funny thing. Them villages was trailin' south an' east. But the other trails are all goin' north an' west. Now what do you reckon is up there to draw 'em all like flies to a honey jar?"

"Hell, I don't know. North and west of here?"

"Yup. Toward the south fork of Hat Creek. Or mebbe toward Rialto Creek. It's like in the old days, when all trails was headin' for rendezvous."

Moya glanced along the parade. The barracks across the way were dark. Taps had sounded more than an hour before. There was a dim light in the sutler's store, but headquarters, the post hospital, and all the other buildings were dark. A solitary lamp burned in Major Burkhalter's quarters and another in Lieutenant Keefe's.

Moya said, "Buy you a drink, Irish?"

"I could use that." O'Rourke headed for the sutler's store, with Moya following.

Moya waited until they had passed headquarters. Then his hand slid his knife from the scabbard at his side. He moved forward, closing with O'Rourke. He put his left hand on O'Rourke's shoulder to steady him, then drove the knife with his right.

O'Rourke grunted with surprise. Moya let go the knife and clapped his right hand over O'Rourke's mouth. He eased the man to the ground, holding him thus until O'Rourke went limp. He withdrew his knife and walked on down to the sutler's store. He cut through the passageway to the little courtyard at the rear of it.

He knelt beside the pump and drove his knife into the wet earth several times to take the blood off the blade. He tamped the earth smooth again with his boot. He raised the knife and peered at the blade in the faint light coming from the back door of the sutler's place. Satisfied, he sheathed it and retraced his steps through the passageway. He went into the front door.

There were two N.C.O.s at the bar. The post trader, Schwarz, was behind it, looking sleepy. He glanced at Moya. "O'Rourke get back?"

Moya nodded. "I offered to buy him a

drink but he said he was tired and wanted to turn in."

Schwarz poured him a three-finger drink of whisky and Moya gulped it down. The two troopers were arguing drunkenly but Moya wasn't listening to their argument. He was listening to the silence of the post, to the silence out there on the parade. He wished one of the sentries, or someone, would find O'Rourke's body, but he knew it was possible it wouldn't be found until tomorrow. If not, he might be accused. But there was another way . . .

He said, "See you to-morrow, Schwarz," got up, and went outside. He walked along the gallery in the direction of headquarters. When he could see O'Rourke's lumped shape, he suddenly yelled, "Hey! Hey, you damned redskin . . . !"

He heard a shout from the gate even as he began to run. He raced back toward the stables, a growing commotion behind him. Fifty feet short of the stables, he suddenly yanked out his revolver and fired a shot into the air and, a few moments later, another one.

He began to curse softly to himself. Sergeant Hochstadt came running across the parade in his underwear. "What is it, man?"

"Injun jumped O'Rourke back there on the parade. Went over the roof of the stable and out that way. I think I winged him but I ain't real sure."

Hochstadt turned and ran back up the parade. Moya followed more slowly. He could see a cluster of men there now, around Kiowa O'Rourke.

He was sorry about killing O'Rourke because he had liked the old Irishman. But he's had no choice. Alive, O'Rourke would have spoiled his plan.

Schwarz, the post trader, caught up with him, running, and slowed to walk beside him. "Thought you said he was going to turn in."

"Must've changed his mind and decided he wanted that drink after all. And that damn' Cheyenne waitin' for him. I wonder if I did wing the son-of-a-bitch."

He began to hurry slightly. He couldn't understand why the men were standing around O'Rourke so long. Why didn't they pick up his body and carry him away?

Keefe heard the shouts only faintly, but the shot was plain and very distinct. He was moving before the second one sounded, running toward the door, slamming it open, and charging out across the gallery onto the parade.

It took several moments before his eyes, accustomed to the lamplight inside his room, became adjusted to the darkness of the parade. In the interval, he heard the second shot and saw the gun flare down there in the direction of the sutler's store. A few moments later, running, he almost stumbled over the body of Kiowa O'Rourke.

He hesitated an instant between charging off in the direction of the shots or staying here and trying to help the scout — if he was not already beyond mortal help. His decision made, he knelt beside O'Rourke.

He was surprised to discover that breath still gusted raggedly from the old scout's lungs. He said anxiously, "O'Rourke. Can you hear me, O'Rourke?"

The reply was a groan. Keefe raised his head and looked around. Other forms were approaching now — from officers' country, from the barracks on the other side of the parade. Keefe yelled, "Get the surgeon, somebody! O'Rourke's been hurt!"

O'Rourke groaned again. Keefe bent closer, having done all he could until the surgeon could arrive. He didn't want to move the wounded man, not until Dr.

Lynch had determined how badly he was hurt.

O'Rourke said, "Lieutenant . . ."

"Yes? Who did this, O'Rourke?"

"Cheyenne . . ." The voice was weak and Keefe had to lean close to hear. ". . . movin'. All movin'." The voice died away. There were other men standing around O'Rourke and Keefe now, talking in shocked, subdued tones. Their talk made it harder for Keefe to hear. He leaned even closer still.

O'Rourke was breathing more harshly now, and very painfully. But Keefe caught the words, "Rialto Creek."

He gripped O'Rourke's shoulder. "What about Rialto Creek? Man, what about Rialto Creek?"

"Trails headin' that way. Like rendezvous. Maybe not Rialto Creek. Maybe Hat Creek instead. Up that way . . ."

"How many trails, O'Rourke?" Keefe realised his fingers were biting into the scout's shoulder. And it was too late. O'Rourke slumped suddenly, going altogether limp. There was no longer any sound of breathing.

The surgeon pushed through the crowd, a lantern in his hand. He knelt beside O'Rourke. Keefe said, "I think it's too late, Dr. Lynch."

Lynch knelt there a moment, holding the old scout's wrist. Then he nodded, rising to his feet. He said, "A couple of you men carry him into the post hospital."

Moya now arrived, with Schwarz, the sutler. Moya asked, "Is he dead?"

Keefe nodded. "You were the one that was yelling and shooting when I came out?"

"Uh huh. There was an Injun bendin' over him. I yelled an' the redskin ran. I thing I might of winged him, but I ain't right sure."

Burkhalter pushed his way through the crowd, his harsh, commanding voice preceding him. "What the hell's all the commotion out here?"

Someone told him that O'Rourke had been killed. Burkhalter, his voice icy with rage, said, "I want to see the officer of the day immediately. And the corporal of the guard. I want to know how a murdering goddamned Indian can get inside this fort!"

Lieutenant DuBois stepped up, saluted, and told Burkhalter he was the officer of the day. Burkhalter ordered him to find the corporal of the guard and report to him immediately at headquarters.

Keefe walked with the surgeon to the post hospital. He followed Dr. Lynch inside.

The surgeon looked questioningly at him. Keefe said, "I'd just like to know what killed him, Dr. Lynch. He said some strange things just before he died."

"Like what, Keefe?"

Keefe frowned, trying to remember O'Rourke's exact words. "Things about the Cheyennes making trails going north — toward Hat Creek, or Rialto Creek."

"Better tell the major what he said."

Keefe nodded. "I will."

The men who had carried O'Rourke in now retired. Lynch went to the table on which the men had laid the scout. He rolled the body partway over, far enough to see the blood-soaked back of his shirt. He pointed to it. "There's your wound. Knife wound I'd say."

"It could have been an Indian then?"

"What do you mean, could have been? Moya saw the son-of-a-bitch. He took a couple of shots at him."

Keefe nodded. "That's right he did, didn't he? Or at least that's what he says."

"You don't believe him?"

"Seems kind of farfetched, doesn't it? If O'Rourke just got back a little while ago, why didn't this Indian attack him outside the post? Why did he wait until O'Rourke was inside the fort?"

"Maybe he didn't catch up with him . . ." Dr. Lynch stopped, apparently realising how unlikely that sounded, realising too how unlikely it was that an Indian would come inside the fort to kill one man. And why O'Rourke?

Keefe was thinking that Moya must have killed O'Rourke.

Moya had met him at the gate, the sentries said, and had walked away into the darkness with him toward the sutler's store.

A sudden horror began to chill Keefe's thoughts. Suppose Rialto Creek was an ambush? That and only that would satisfactorily explain all that had happened tonight. It would explain the trails O'Rourke had found heading northwest toward the place. It would explain Moya's killing him, if indeed Moya had, because if Moya had planned an ambush with the Cheyennes he would certainly not let O'Rourke give it away.

Keefe said shakily, "I think I had better talk to Major Burkhalter. Right away." And he bolted for the door.

CHAPTER 10

Several lamps were burning at headquarters. The whole fort was lighted up. Across the parade, enlisted men were gathered in groups, talking over what had happened to

O'Rourke.

Keefe stepped into headquarters as Burkhalter was dismissing DuBois. The lieutenant's face was deeply flushed with embarrassment and anger. The corporal of the guard slunk out ahead of him.

Keefe went to the open door of Burkhalter's office and knocked. Burkhalter snarled, "What the hell is it now?"

Keefe went in. He said, "I reached O'Rourke first, Major Burkhalter. I thought you ought to know what his last words were."

"He wasn't dead?" Burkhalter looked up, eyes narrowed, his face blank with surprise.

"No, sir. He wasn't dead, and I talked to him."

"Go on, man. Go on!"

Keefe nodded. "I'm trying to remember his exact words . . . He said 'Cheyenne . . .' "

"Likely he meant that a Cheyenne killed him. That confirms what Moya said."

"I don't think so, Major. Not considering what came next. He said, 'Cheyenne . . . movin'. All movin' '."

"Of course they're moving. Moya told us that. It's what I expected them to do."

"Yes, sir. But he said something else. He said, 'Rialto Creek or maybe Hat Creek. Trails all heading up that way. Like rendezvous'."

Burkhalter peered at Keefe, squinting because of the lamp on the desk in front of him. "Do you mean to stand there and tell me that he said all that? And then died? And that you're the only man who heard him say anything? DuBois and Corporal Delaney both said that he was dead when they got to him."

Keefe was stunned but he was also furious. "Are you accusing me of lying to you, sir? What possible reason could I have for telling you this if it wasn't true?"

Burkhalter met his angry glance steadily. "I am trying to figure that out, mister. I am trying to figure that one out."

Keefe saluted, his face white, his mouth compressed with rage. He turned to leave, but Burkhalter snapped, "You have not been dismissed, Lieutenant Keefe! You will stand at attention until you are!"

"Yes, sir!" Keefe snapped to rigid attention, staring straight ahead, looking at a spot on the wall behind Burkhalter. He was being treated like a brand-new shavetail just out of West Point. Worse, he had been bluntly accused of lying.

Burkhalter's voice was softly furious. "I have not missed your behaviour with my wife, Lieutenant, the way you have ingrati-

111

ated yourself with her. I have not missed the way you have been all sympathy with the Shores. You do not approve of me or of my campaign against the Indians, do you, Lieutenant Keefe?"

"I am not required to approve or to disapprove, sir. I am a junior officer who has just arrived. It would be presumptuous of me." Keefe held himself ramrod stiff, speaking as he once had to upperclassmen at West Point.

"Damn you, Keefe, don't use that tone with me!"

"Yes, sir. No, sir." Keefe shifted his glance to Burkhalter's face. It was a brick-red, a dark, dangerous-looking red. The veins stood out prominently on Burkhalter's forehead. Keefe said, "I'm sorry, sir. I only came to tell you what O'Rourke said before he died. I thought it was my duty to tell you, sir. I still think it was."

"You're a liar, Keefe. And don't think I don't know why you had yourself transferred to Kettering. You're here to revenge yourself against me for what happened to your father during the war."

Keefe clenched his fists, held so rigidly at his sides. He didn't know how much more of this he was going to be able to take, but he knew the major wasn't through with him.

Burkhalter wanted him to attack him physically . . . and if he did, the major would see to it that he was hanged . . . or shot.

Burkhalter's voice was even softer than it had been before, but it was charged with tension. "It won't work, Keefe. It won't work. I do not intend to leave you here at Fort Kettering with Mrs. Burkhalter when I take the field against the Indians. There have been men who hated me in my command before, Lieutenant Keefe. There have been other attempts to shoot me in the back and I am not afraid of you."

Keefe stared at him, aghast. "Surely you don't think that I . . ."

"Would shoot me in the back? Of course I believe it, Keefe. I also happen to believe that if I leave you behind, you will do your best to seduce my wife."

Keefe's anger was ebbing now before the horror that was slowly but surely crowding it aside. Burkhalter was out of his mind, he thought. Burkhalter was completely mad! He realised that Burkhalter's office door was still open. This insane exchange was being overheard. By morning it would be all over the post.

He wondered what he should do. Should he try making a calm, reasonable denial of Burkhalter's charges? Or should he keep his mouth shut, hoping the major would dismiss him if he did?

He decided to try persuading Burkhalter that he was wrong. He said, "You're mistaken about me, sir. I didn't come here for revenge. As for your wife . . ." He stopped, aware of how delicate the subject was. At last, knowing he must say something since he had brought the subject up, he said, "I could do nothing but go after her when I saw her go out the gate."

For several moments Burkhalter was silent. Keefe could hear him breathing heavily.

At last Burkhalter said in a more normal voice, "You will not repeat the lies you have told me to my other officers. You will not undermine their confidence with falsehoods. Is that clear, Lieutenant Keefe?"

Once more Keefe's anger soared. He clenched his jaws and at last said tightly, "I will repeat no lies, sir. You have my word."

"Then you're dismissed."

Keefe saluted stiffly. He turned on his heel and marched from the office. He slammed out the door, almost colliding with an enlisted man who had been standing there listening.

He gestured with his head angrily and the trooper preceded him along the gallery.

When Keefe judged they were out of Burkhalter's hearing, he asked angrily, "What's your name, trooper?"

"Brown, sir. Lance corporal, K Troop."

Keefe spoke between clenched teeth. "Let me tell you something, Trooper Brown. If anything you have overheard is repeated to anyone, you will have a court-martial to look forward to. Is that clear?"

Brown's face was white and scared. "Yes, sir."

"Then get out of here!"

"Yes, sir!" Brown trotted off across the parade.

Keefe strode along the gallery toward his quarters, which he had left so precipitously when he heard the commotion on the parade. He almost hoped Mrs. Burkhalter's door would be open and that she would call to him. But it was closed.

He went on past and slammed into his room, banging the door so hard that dust sifted from the ceiling immediately over it. He stared furiously at nothing for a moment, then saw the bottle and glasses on the commode.

He poured himself half a tumbler full and gulped it furiously. He poured another half glass, crossed the room, and put it down. He sat on the bed, took a cigar from his tunic, bit off the end, and lighted it.

Damn Burkhalter! He gulped the whisky, got up, and poured himself some more. There was a burning sensation in his throat and stomach. His head was beginning to feel just a little light.

This was a situation the like of which he had never encountered before. He did not know how to cope with it. But he had an uneasy feeling that if he did not find a way to cope with it he was going to be destroyed. He was going to be destroyed as his father had been destroyed.

At seven the next morning, carefully dressed and wearing grim but frightened expressions, Nathan and Mrs. Shore presented themselves at headquarters and asked Corporal Ord to tell Major Burkhalter they wished to speak to him.

Scowling, unshaven, looking as though he had not slept, Burkhalter came out of his office and stood looking coldly down at them. "Good morning, Mr. Shore."

"Good morning, Major. We would like to return to Omaha, if you will arrange escort for us."

Burkhalter shrugged. He looked at Ord. "Tell the sergeant who escorted Mr. and

Mrs. Shore here to make ready to return at once."

Ord went out. Burkhalter looked irritably at Shore. "Was there something else?"

Shore swallowed. His eyes were frightened, but they were determined too. He said, "You killed our son, Major Burkhalter. You killed him as surely as if you had pulled the trigger yourself. Until you attacked that village on Cut Nose Creek, the Cheyennes were peaceable."

Burkhalter turned and strode into his office. He returned with a handful of dry scalps, one grey, one light brown, one small and blond. He threw them contemptuously down on Corporal Ord's desk. "Peaceable, Mr. Shore? Peaceful Indians do not take scalps from settlers. Particularly from children of that age."

Mrs. Shore looked as though she were going to be ill. She sat down suddenly. Shore glanced at her, then back at the major. "Those are not fresh scalps, Major Burkhalter. They could be several years old."

"Who the hell told you that?"

Shore flushed slightly. "I have been talking to your men."

"Who? By God, give me their names and . . . !"

"I will not give you any names. We just

know one thing, Major Burkhalter. You have killed our son."

"And what do you think you're going to do about this wild idea of yours?"

"We will talk to General Stiles in Omaha. We will talk to the newspapers. We will talk to anyone that will listen to us. Perhaps as a result you will be removed from your command, from all command. Then maybe you will not be able to kill any more boys like ours."

Shore was trembling violently. Mrs. Shore had begun to cry. Corporal Ord returned. He saluted the major and said, "They'll be ready in half an hour, sir." He looked puzzledly from the Shores to the major and back again.

Major Burkhalter was livid. His fist slammed down like a hammer against the desk. "Get out of here, sir! Get out! Get out of here and don't come back! I will not have civilians telling me how to run my command. Get out!"

Shore took his wife's arm and the two hurried fearfully out. Burkhalter scowled after them a moment, then went into his office and slammed the door thunderously.

Holding on to each other, almost as though for support, the Shores hurried to their quarters. Their luggage had been piled on the gallery. They waited fearfully for the wagon that had brought them here.

Mrs. Shore began to cry again. Nathan Shore continued to tremble from the scene he'd had with Burkhalter. He put an arm around his wife and patted her shoulder awkwardly. "We should not have come, Mother. It would have been better if we had never known for sure."

The wagon and escort rattled across the parade. It stopped beside the Shores and the driver helped Mr. Shore to load their bags. The old man helped his wife up, then climbed up after her. The wagon rattled away toward the gates, which were opened to let them through. The escort followed the wagon outside, splitting then, four in front of the wagon, four behind.

Escort and wagon dusted slowly along the road until they were lost to sight.

CHAPTER 11

Keefe heard Major Burkhalter shouting intemperately at the Shores down at head-quarters. He heard them walk hurriedly past his door. From his window he watched them load their bags, climb to the seat of the light wagon, and drive out of the fort, the eight man escort trotting their horses along behind.

He had a thunderous headache this morning and his mouth tasted cottony, but along with the hangover he was feeling something infinitely worse, a gloomy premonition of disaster and a realisation of his helplessness. There was but one way to add up what O'Rourke had seen during his scout south of Fort Kettering, but Burkhalter would not believe. So badly did he want to wipe out another village that he simply refused to face the truth.

The truth was that Moya, not a Cheyenne brave, had killed O'Rourke last night. Of that Keefe was very sure. Moya had killed O'Rourke to keep him from reporting to Burkhalter what he had told Keefe before he died — that every trail he had found was headed straight for the village on Rialto Creek.

It took no brilliant tactician to interpret the meaning of all those converging trails. The village on Rialto Creek was a set and baited trap. When Burkhalter's forces attacked it, they would be attacked in turn from the rear by every Cheyenne brave within a radius of a hundred miles.

Scowling, Keefe paced restlessly back and forth. Then, cursing softly to himself, he put on his hat and went out onto the gallery. Squinting against the nearly blinding rays of the morning sun, he stood still for a moment, then turned and walked deliberately along the gallery toward the officers' mess.

MacPhee glanced up at him as he came in and glanced away immediately, suppressing a faint smile. Keefe got himself a cup of coffee and sat down. He considered risking Burkhalter's wrath by telling MacPhee what O'Rourke had said before he died, but then he shook his head. Not yet, he thought. Not this morning. Not when his head was pounding so mercilessly he could scarcely think. If he was going to succeed in making MacPhee believe his story, he would need all his wits about him.

DuBois came in and sat down beside him. The lieutenant's dark, narrow face was still chagrined. He looked at Keefe and smiled ruefully. "I heard him yelling at you last night too. What was he chewing you out about?"

Keefe couldn't tell DuBois what his argument with Burkhalter had been about. Part of that he would never tell anybody. So he muttered, "General principles, I guess."

"Still mad at me, I suppose. He was chewing me out when you came in."

MacPhee said dryly, "An Indian *did* get

inside the fort. An Indian *did* get past the sentries, gentlemen."

DuBois raised an eyebrow questioningly. "Did he, Captain? All we have is Joe Moya's word for that. No one else saw an Indian. There was no blood on the roof where Moya said he disappeared. There were no tracks where O'Rourke's body was found."

MacPhee stopped eating and stared at him. "What are you trying to say? That Moya killed O'Rourke?"

"No. I'm not trying to say that. I don't know what I think. I don't know what *to* think."

MacPhee looked at Keefe. "You reached O'Rourke first, Lieutenant Keefe. Did he say anything to you, or was he dead when you got to him?"

Keefe evaded. "He said a few things that didn't seem to make much sense. I'll try to remember them when my head's a little clearer than it is right now."

He noticed the surgeon studying him. MacPhee was also looking at him carefully. He didn't know what any of them could do even if he did tell what O'Rourke had said, even if they did believe as he did, that an ambush was waiting at Rialto Creek. Burkhalter was still the commandant. They would do what Burkhalter ordered them to do, even if it meant riding straight into a Cheyenne trap.

Dr. Lynch spoke now, looking puzzledly at Keefe. "Last night you said something about O'Rourke finding Indian trails going north — toward Hat Creek or Rialto Creek."

MacPhee's glance sharpened. "I think you had better tell me exactly what O'Rourke did say, Lieutenant Keefe."

"That was about it, Captain. He murmured something about trails going north — like rendezvous, he said."

"Toward Rialto Creek?"

"Yes, sir. Or Hat Creek. I guess they're both up that way."

"What are you thinking, Keefe? That Moya may have killed O'Rourke? That he has a trap set for us on Rialto Creek?"

"I don't know what to think, sir. I don't know Moya and I didn't know O'Rourke. But there's something smelly here and I think we ought to be aware of it."

"Did you tell Major Burkhalter all this?"

Keefe felt his face flushing. He nodded.

"And?"

"He accused me of lying, sir."

MacPhee nodded. "All right, Keefe. I'll talk to you about it again later on."

Keefe nodded. He finished his coffee,

glanced at the food, and looked weakly away, then got up and left the room. On the gallery, he lighted a cigar, fighting his nausea.

Half a dozen hayracks were creaking across the parade toward the gates. A ten man mounted escort followed them. The men of the haying detail rode on one of the hayracks, sitting cross-legged in a circle, playing cards on the uneven floor.

Across the parade in front of K Troop's barracks, Keefe saw the scout Joe Moya talking with several troopers. He was pointing toward the stable where he had claimed the Indian disappeared. Retelling the story, thought Keefe. Perpetuating the lie. But how the hell was anyone going to prove it was a lie?

A bugler blew officers' call. Keefe joined the others and walked toward headquarters. He hoped Burkhalter wouldn't notice his bloodshot eyes, his obvious hangover, but he supposed that was too much to hope for. At least, maybe the major wouldn't comment on it.

Burkhalter was waiting for them. He said, "Take seats, gentlemen. You may smoke."

Keefe sat down behind Captain MacPhee. When the room had quieted, Burkhalter said, "As you all probably know by now,

O'Rourke was murdered here inside the fort by a Cheyenne Indian last night. That means we will have but one scout when we move against the Cheyenne village on Rialto Creek."

Nobody spoke. Burkhalter asked, "How are your preparations coming, gentlemen? Captain Leighton?"

"K Troop is ready, sir."

"MacPhee?"

"Both L and B Troops are ready, sir."

"We will move out at dawn. Reveille will be at four, breakfast at four-thirty. Are there any questions?"

MacPhee stood up. "Yes, sir. What about the intelligence that O'Rourke brought back?"

Burkhalter's face began to grow red. "What intelligence, Captain MacPhee?"

"About the trails heading for Rialto Creek."

Burkhalter stared murderously at Keefe. "I believe I told you not to repeat those lies, Lieutenant Keefe."

MacPhee interrupted stoutly. "Lies, Major? What reason do we have for believing Lieutenant Keefe would make up lies? As a matter of fact, he talked to Dr. Lynch last night before he talked with you. Dr. Lynch was the one who mentioned O'Rourke's last words."

"Are you defending Keefe?" Burkhalter's face was pale now, his eyes like bits of stone.

"Why yes, sir, I suppose I am. Lieutenant Keefe has been assigned to my troop." MacPhee held Burkhalter's furious glance steadily and it was Burkhalter who finally looked away.

For a long time the major stared stonily at the ceiling above his head. At last he said, "That is all, gentlemen."

They got up silently and filed outside. All except MacPhee. He stayed and when he and Burkhalter were alone he said, "I'd like to question Moya, sir."

"Permission denied. He is the only scout we have and he's touchy. I won't have him antagonised. Besides, suppose Keefe's story is the truth? Suppose that village on Rialto Creek is somewhat bigger than Moya said it was? We can handle it. It will only give us a bigger victory."

MacPhee stared at him a moment. "Sam, for God's sake . . ."

Burkhalter's face did not soften. "That is all, Captain MacPhee. You may go."

MacPhee saluted. "Yes, sir." He swung around and went outside.

Burkhalter stared after him. He turned

126

and went into his office and closed the door. He walked to the window and stared outside, scowling angrily. He was thinking of Martha and remembering all the men she had found interesting in the five years since he had married her. Damn her! God damn her anyway! He ought to throw her out. He ought to wring her neck. But he didn't intend doing anything that would cause a scandal. He didn't intend to let anything jeopardise his chances of getting his general's star back again.

He began to pace nervously back and forth. His eyes began to gleam with a fierce kind of eagerness. He hadn't felt like this since the end of the war, more than five years ago. By God he would be a general again. He would! He'd show Martha! He'd show them all!

Lieutenant Keefe walked thoughtfully along the gallery, heading toward his quarters. He frowned slightly to himself, remembering the way Burkhalter had looked at him a few moments before.

Burkhalter hated him, hated him savagely. His look had made that very plain if his words earlier had not.

The big question in Keefe's mind right now was why. He'd done nothing since coming here to deserve that kind of hatred. There had been nothing of any consequence between him and the major's wife and what had been between them was her doing, not his. Besides, Burkhalter knew what she was. The lieutenant Keefe had replaced had been transferred because of Mrs. Burkhalter. So the major's hatred couldn't be because of her.

His frown deepened. It had to be because of his father, then. It had to be because Burkhalter was afraid.

A strange tension began to grow in Keefe. If Burkhalter was afraid of him, afraid of his presence here, then certainly it proved that Burkhalter and not his father had been to blame at Indian Creek. Burkhalter was afraid he was going to try to reopen the case. The major feared his doing so would jeopardise his chances for promotion.

The strange, uneasy premonition he had felt earlier now returned. Regaining his general's stars was an obsession with Major Burkhalter. For them he was willing to start an Indian war out here on the plains. He was willing to sacrifice as many men of his command as were necessary. He did not, apparently, care how many settlers were murdered by the Indians in retaliation for his savagery.

Burkhalter was a type, Keefe thought uneasily. A military type. A man steeped in tactical thinking until he has lost sight of human values, a man who played at war the way others play at chess, sacrificing living men the way a chess player sacrifices his chessmen in order to win. Burkhalter would never have trouble convincing himself that what he did was for the best, a necessity of war, a price to be paid for military victory. At Indian Creek he had jumped the gun, attacking too soon, with the result, even though he took the bluff, that he lost twice as many men as would have been lost otherwise.

Keefe reached the door to his quarters and stepped inside, surprised to find the door ajar. He stopped, and froze, just inside. Swiftly, then, he closed the door behind him and put his back to it.

Martha Burkhalter was in the room. Keefe said furiously, "Do you know what your husband would do to me if anyone were to see you here?"

Her face was pale, her eyes enormous and filled with fright. For the briefest instant he was sorry for her but when he remembered how brazenly she had offered herself to him, his pity evaporated. She whispered, "I'm sorry, Lieutenant. But I had to see you. I had to warn you."

"About what?" He stared at her suspiciously.

"About my husband. He does not intend that you return from the village on Rialto Creek. You are to be a casualty."

He stared unbelievingly. His heart nearly stopped as he heard footsteps approaching along the gallery. He held his breath until they reached his door, until they had gone on past. He said, "You must be insane."

"No, Lieutenant. I'm not insane. But my husband is. I know that you do not think very highly of me and I suppose I cannot blame you for that, but I am telling you the truth. If you go with him to-morrow, you will not return."

Keefe heard footsteps approaching again. They halted and a knock sounded on the door.

Keefe felt the blood drain from his face. His knees felt weak. He didn't know who it could be outside, but if anyone found Martha Burkhalter here . . .

He cleared his throat and said, "Just a minute." He waved her urgently aside so that she would not be visible when he opened the door. Then he opened it and stepped out onto the gallery.

Captain MacPhee was standing there. He

stared at Keefe's face and Keefe had the frightening feeling that MacPhee could literally read his thoughts. MacPhee said, "I want you down at headquarters, Keefe. There are some details I want to go over with you."

"Yes, sir."

"What's the matter, Keefe? You look kind of sick."

Keefe made a sickly smile. "I guess I overdid it a bit last night, sir, after my run-in with Major Burkhalter."

MacPhee nodded, but Keefe could see he did not entirely accept the explanation. MacPhee stared at the closed door a moment as though trying to pierce it with his glance. Then, abruptly, he turned and walked along the gallery.

Keefe followed. He felt as though a ball of ice was in his chest. It was broad daylight. How was Martha Burkhalter going to leave his quarters without being seen?

Another thought made him begin to sweat. Suppose she had been seen going in?

CHAPTER 12

The remainder of the day was a busy one. Two ambulances were to go along tomorrow. There was to be one ammunition wagon and two supply wagons, and these had to be loaded and made ready.

Ammunition was issued to the men. Each man examined his own horse carefully, looking at each shoe, having the animals reshod when necessary. All day smoke rose from the two forges at the blacksmith shop. All day there was a line of horses outside waiting to be shod.

There was an indefinable air of excitement about the post to-day, one with which those who had served in the war were familiar. It was pre-battle excitement. Few of the men at Kettering believed the village on Rialto Creek would be as easy as the one on Cut Nose Creek had been. The Cheyennes were alert now. They probably even had scouts watching the fort.

Near sundown the hay wagons returned. And to-night, taps was earlier than usual by an hour and a half.

At the end of the day, Keefe returned to his quarters, half afraid that he would still find Martha Burkhalter there, but he did not. Nothing remained to show that she had been there at all. Yet Keefe's uneasiness persisted. He could not believe she could have come and gone in broad daylight without being seen. Sooner or later someone who had seen her would talk. And then all hell was going to break loose.

Lieutenant Hargreaves limped in on crutches a little before taps. He grinned weakly at Keefe. "Wish I was going with you to-morrow."

Keefe nodded but he did not reply. The uneasy premonition had remained with him all day. He was certain the village on Rialto Creek was a trap. He was sure the command would be slaughtered by the Indians. He examined his own feelings with some care, trying to decide if he was afraid to die and admitted that he was. He supposed every man was afraid to die. The trick was not to let it show — or give way to it.

Martha Burkhalter had said her husband did not intend to let him return alive to Fort Kettering. He wondered if Burkhalter would actually try killing him. The man was capable of it, of course. There was no doubt in his mind of that. Burkhalter would shoot him as readily as he would shoot any enemy that threatened him.

Hargreaves was weary from the exertion of leaving the hospital, so both men turned in early. Lying in bed, staring into the darkness, Keefe was tense with pre-battle excitement in spite of his certainty that only defeat waited for the command. But he also discovered in himself an odd nostalgia, a strange ability to remember things from long ago with startling clarity.

He thought of his father and for the first time in years seemed to see his father's face clearly, strong, bearded, virile, and alive. Looking that way before the battle of Indian Creek. He remembered the way it had been afterward as vividly — confused, defeated, sometimes angry with helplessness.

Suddenly Keefe realised how very angry he had always been at the injustice of it all. He realised something else, admitted it to himself for the first time. Revenge *had* been his motive when he asked for assignment to Fort Kettering. The hunger for it had lain smouldering in the back of his mind these many years.

Burkhalter deserved to die, not only for what he had done to Rufus Keefe, but also for those dead unnecessarily on the bluff overlooking Indian Creek. He deserved to die for the murdered Indians at Cut Nose Creek, for Private Isaac Shore, for the settlers tortured and dead because the Cheyennes had struck out blindly at them in revenge.

He deserved to die and Martin Keefe had reason for killing him, yet suddenly, tonight, he knew that he would not revenge himself that way. Never could he shed his training and principles sufficiently to kill another man in cold blood, particularly not his commanding officer. Everything he had learned in four years at West Point, everything innately decent in him found only disgust in the thought of it. If Samuel Burkhalter died it would not be by Keefe's hand.

He slept, finally, but it was not an easy sleep. Through his dreams paraded Joe Moya and Kiowa O'Rourke, Martha Burkhalter and the major. Moya was throttling the major and Keefe was trying to pull him off but there was no strength in him and even in his dreams he realised he was as guilty as Moya was because he wasn't really trying to pull Moya off until the job was done.

He awoke, sweating, to hear the last notes of reveille running along the length of the parade. He got up and for several moments sat on the edge of the bed with his head in his hands. The dream had been very real and still seemed so and it was not hard for him to understand what it meant. He could kill Burkhalter by failure to act just as surely as he could kill him by direct action, and he would not know until the time for it came what he would do. That was to be his burden of uncertainty on the campaign.

He got to his feet and dressed swiftly, then looked at his arms and his gear. He crammed his hat down on his head and poked his head into Hargreaves's room. "See you in a week, Hargreaves."

"Good luck, Keefe."

"Thanks." Keefe went out into the pre-dawn darkness. He hurried along the gallery toward the officers' mess.

There was a lamp burning in Burkhalter's quarters. Passing, Keefe could not help thinking of Martha, could not help feeling sorry for her. She was a troublemaker whose eye was out for any unattached male anywhere near her age, but, married to Burkhalter, such behaviour was not difficult to understand. Burkhalter's whole life was one of consuming ambition. The past five years, those since the end of the war, had been years of frustration and defeat for him. Not qualities and pressures that make a man easy for a woman to live with, Keefe thought wryly. And there was also the fact that Burkhalter was more than twice her age.

He reached the officers' mess. Across the parade, men were shouting at each other boisterously. Down at the stables horses kicked and squealed, and across the parade, wagons squeaked as they were drawn out into line.

Among the officers there was restrained talk, good-natured joking, and more laughter than usual. Lieutenant Mills, who was staying behind because of his wife's illness, was almost pathetically disappointed and showed it in spite of his efforts to keep it concealed.

Breakfast was soon over. A bugler sounded "boots and saddles" and the din of commotion grew almost deafening. Slowly order emerged out of chaos and two troops and part of a third formed on the parade, facing headquarters.

Keefe swung a leg over his mount and followed Captain MacPhee up the greying parade to take his place in front of L Troop. Suddenly the men were silent, and the horses too, and a hush fell over all the fort.

Burkhalter waved his sabre and shouted. The command "Count off!" rang down along the line, followed after the count by "Left by twos!" and the executing command, recognisable only as "Ho-o-o-o!"

The troopers moved, swinging left by twos, forming a column with officers and guidon bearers leading each troop toward the gate. Keefe glanced right and saw Martha Burkhalter standing in her doorway watching him. It was too dark to tell what her expression was and she did not move, yet he had the feeling there were tears in her eyes. Tears for whom he could not guess, for Burkhalter, for him, for herself, or perhaps for all three of them.

Out through the gates they went, and behind them the ponderous things swung shut, and the fort went about its daily humdrum routine but with a little more watchfulness because now it was dangerously undermanned.

Ahead, above the river and the river bluffs, the sun turned the sky to violet, then pink, then to a golden shade and immediately after that it rose, a dazzling ball seeming to emerge from one of the ponds the beavers had made in the distance along the Platte. Strong now was the smell of sage, crushed by the horses' hooves. Strong was the smell of dust, and of leather, and of the horses themselves. The wagons rolled down the steep road off the river bluff, canting dangerously it seemed sometimes, but easing back and forth over the switchbacks in the road until they were splashing across the river ford and climbing out on the other side.

Burkhalter rode in the lead, Joe Moya beside him, his face as impassive as if it had been carved from stone. Moya's voice when he spoke was pleasant enough, but his eyes, hooded and slitted, never warmed and never smiled. Once the Platte was crossed, Burkhalter put out flankers, and Joe Moya dropped back, alone, to look for Cheyenne scouts. Discovering none, he galloped to the head of the column once more, raised a hand to wave at the major, and trotted on ahead.

He drew rein atop a low rise a mile and a half ahead of the crawling column and looked back. He could see the flankers a quarter mile to the right and left of the column. He could make out the hulking and solitary figure of Burkhalter in the lead. He could see the wagons crawling, and the thin dust bannering out to the windward of the trotting horses' hooves.

There had been some kind of fuss among the officers over the death of O'Rourke night before last, and both yesterday and this morning there had been cool looks directed toward him by several of them. He smiled grimly to himself. Burkhalter's greed to kill and his greed to recover his general's star had prevailed over their cautioning. Half the men in the post had heard Burkhalter shouting at Lieutenant Keefe but the preparations for this expedition had gone ahead.

He found himself thinking about Lieutenant Keefe and wondering exactly what Keefe had heard from O'Rourke before the old scout died. Perhaps whatever he had heard had not been too readily understandable. At least Burkhalter had refused to believe. Moya grinned. Burkhalter might not even have believed O'Rourke.

He was sorry about Keefe, who'd had nothing to do with the Cut Nose massacre. He was sorry that Keefe had to die. But pity was a luxury he could not allow himself. It wasn't hard to remember the carnage at Cut Nose Creek whenever pity threatened to intrude upon his thoughts. It wasn't hard to remember the cold, smooth face of Red Earth Woman, or the stiffening, cold bodies of the children, innocent victims too.

He touched heels to his horse's sides and moved ahead. He watched the ground, but he saw no trails. Nor was it likely that he would, not yet at least. This column was heading straight toward the village on Rialto Creek. All the other trails would be heading for the same place, converging like the spokes of a wagon wheel at the hub. None of the trails would meet until they reached Rialto Creek.

Scouting was what he had signed on to do, though, even if he didn't find anything. So he rode ahead, and he kept a wary eye peeled for the Cheyenne scouts he knew could not be far away. They probably had orders from Tall Elk not to molest him, but he wasn't going to stake his life on their obedience.

The command would camp to-night a little over half-way to Rialto Creek. It would camp to-morrow night a scant dozen miles away from it, and hit it at dawn on the day following.

Then Moya would have his vengeance, which now seemed so sweet to anticipate. He did not think of what would happen afterwards. He did not stop to realise that he, too, would probably be killed.

He did not think of what he would do if he lived. There was nothing left for which he wanted to continue life. Red Earth Woman was dead. She was dead, dead . . . There was nothing left but vengeance.

CHAPTER 13

Five officers and two hundred and twenty-seven men. One scout and five canvas-topped wagons, each drawn by four tough army mules. Joe Moya came riding back in late afternoon, reined his horse around beside Major Burkhalter, and made a casual salute, a gesture of raising hand to hat brim.

"Couple miles farther on, Major, we cross a low divide. There's water and good grass on the other side. We'll be there afore sundown."

Burkhalter nodded shortly, studying Moya with more care than he ever had before. The scout pretended not to notice his scrutiny, frowning slightly and staring straight ahead with narrowed eyes.

Burkhalter wondered fleetingly if Moya *had* killed O'Rourke the other night. It was possible, of course, but he didn't really believe it. There seemed to be no reason why the scout should want O'Rourke dead. Keefe's story of trails going north was pure poppycock, a lie concocted for Lord knew what reason, but a lie all the same. Moya had no reason to lead the command into a trap. It didn't make good sense.

Burkhalter hipped around in his saddle and stared back at his command. They were tough frontier soldiers, nearly all of them. Two-thirds had seen service in the Civil War. They'd fight. They'd fight well against any enemy. They could take on two or three times their number and still come out on top. Burkhalter was convinced of it. They could win against a force of six or seven hundred Cheyennes and it was damned unlikely such a force could have been assembled since the battle at Cut Nose Creek.

He himself headed B Troop, at less than half its normal strength, without the assistance of a junior officer since both Hargreaves and Mills had been left behind. Keefe rode at the head of L Troop beside Captain MacPhee and, farther back, DuBois and Leighton rode together at the head of K Troop, bringing up the rear.

A long and dusty column, the command climbed a long rise to the divide Moya had mentioned and descended an equally long slope to a thick grove of trees at the bottom, more than a mile beyond the crest. The flankers came in and the troop executed a column left, then a right by twos, and halted in a line facing the green and cool-looking grove of trees.

Each troop was dismounted and dismissed. Picket lines were established in the trees, but since it was still light, the loose horses were driven out onto the slope to graze under the watchful eyes of a dozen mounted guards. Later, just before dark, they would be driven into a rope corral in the trees, caught again, and tied on the picket line for the night.

Troopers gathered wood, and built fires, and boiled their coffee and cooked their bacon. There was tension among them to-night, the nervous tension of men looking forward to battle, yet somehow fearing it as well. They laughed too much, and joked too much. A few of them just sat and stared moodily into the flames.

Lieutenant Keefe washed in the stream below camp, then returned and squatted beside the fire his orderly had built. The coffee was on, but not yet hot, so he took a cigar from his pocket, bit off the end, and lighted it. He stared into the flames, the sounds of the bivouac a comforting background for his thoughts.

Perhaps the command was riding into a trap. If it was, there was nothing he could do. He had done everything he could. He raised his head and looked around, and was suddenly glad he was a soldier, glad for this life that satisfied him as no other ever would.

He heard a step behind him and glanced up. He saw Lieutenant DuBois staring down at him with sombre face and eyes. He rose and reached for a cigar, but DuBois shook his head. "I want to talk to you. Privately."

"All right." He waved at the slope beyond the trees with his cigar. "Let's walk over there."

He stepped across the narrow stream, with DuBois following. The two strode through the long prairie grass. DuBois glanced nervously over his shoulder before he said, "I'm worried, Keefe. We're riding straight into a trap and Burkhalter knows it and doesn't seem to care. I think he's lost his mind. I don't think he's responsible."

Keefe stopped and stared at him. "That's pretty damn' strong talk."

DuBois stared back defiantly. "Maybe it is, but by God it's true! You told him what O'Rourke said, didn't you? Did he pay any attention to it? Did he even try to check it to see if it was true?"

Keefe shook his head. "No, but that doesn't mean that he's insane."

"He's disobeying a direct order from General Stiles. A man would have to be insane to do a thing like that."

Keefe shrugged. "Why are you telling me? What do you think should be done?"

"I think the two of us ought to talk to Leighton and MacPhee. We've got to make them see."

"And if they do?"

DuBois stared at him defiantly. "Commanders have been relieved of their commands before."

Keefe whistled softly. "Not in the field, DuBois, and not by subordinates. You're suggesting mutiny. We could all get hanged for that."

"I thought . . ." DuBois stopped, his face flushing suddenly with embarrassment.

Keefe peered closely at him. "You thought I hated him?" He smiled slightly. "I suppose I do. I hate him for what he is, for what he did at Cut Nose Creek, and for what he's about to do up north. I hate him for what he did to my father during the war. But that has nothing to do with this." He frowned to himself, staring at the ground. Then he looked up at DuBois. "I would be the worst one you could find to go with you to Leighton and MacPhee. Both of them know about Burkhalter and my father. You'll have a better chance if you go to them alone."

"But you will support what we decide?"

Keefe shook his head. "I suppose I would have no other choice if it was the decision of Captain MacPhee and Leighton to relieve him of his command. I am subordinate to both of them, but . . ." He continued to shake his head. "No, DuBois, I guess even then I would have to oppose the plan. On principle."

"On what grounds, for God's sake? What principle?"

"That mutiny is worse than the condition it is designed to correct."

"Even if we are riding into a trap? Even if

the whole command is going to be slaughtered by the Indians?"

Keefe nodded. "Even then."

DuBois stared at him disgustedly. "You're a fool, Keefe, if you let him drive you to slaughter like a goddam sheep."

"Maybe."

DuBois turned and stalked back to the bivouac. Keefe saw him stop beside Leighton and begin talking with him. Walking slowly, Keefe returned, stepped across the creek, and walked to the fire he had left a few moments before. Bacon was sizzling there, and coffee was boiling. He sat down on a section of fallen log not far from the fire and sipped the coffee the orderly poured for him. After a while Captain MacPhee joined him and the orderly brought them plates of bacon, biscuits and preserves. MacPhee asked, "What did DuBois want?"

Keefe grinned faintly. "I'm not sure I have the right to violate his confidence."

MacPhee grinned back. "I believe I know. He wants to see Burkhalter relieved of his command."

"How did you know that?"

"Things he has said. Did he convince you it was the thing to do?"

Keefe slowly shook his head. "No. I told the major the truth about the things

147

O'Rourke said before he died and I believe we may be riding into a trap. But I don't see that we have much choice. He is the commanding officer. His subordinates don't have the right to mutiny simply because they question his judgment. Or even because they question the motives that make him do the things he does."

MacPhee said slowly, very softly, "He saw Mrs. Burkhalter leaving your quarters the other day. He told me so."

Keefe glanced sharply at him. MacPhee wasn't looking at him. Keefe said, "She was not there at my invitation, Captain. And nothing happened. I give you my word."

MacPhee looked up, met his glance squarely a moment, then nodded almost reluctantly. "You have convinced me, Keefe, but you will never succeed in convincing him. He may even try to kill you at Rialto Creek. I hope you realise that."

Keefe nodded. "I realise it, sir."

MacPhee nodded somewhat wearily. He finished eating and put down his plate. He got up, walked to the fire, and refilled his coffee cup. Returning, he put it down at his feet, then fished in his pocket for a cigar. Keefe, staring at him, felt something close to a chill run along his spine.

There was something bleak and hopeless

in MacPhee's seamed face, as though the captain knew he was going to die, as though he knew this would be his last campaign. Keefe felt a flash of admiration for the man. The premonition was there but MacPhee would certainly never flinch. Nor would he support a mutiny that might save his life.

Keefe got up and walked to the fire. He stared down into its leaping flames for a long, long time. The sun settled behind the western horizon, its glow dying reluctantly afterward. All the colours of sky and land faded into greys that deepened gradually into the black of night.

One by one the fires died to coals that were, in turn, covered with grey ash that hid their glow. The sentries were relieved and the men slept, some fitfully and uneasily, some deeply without moving, some loudly snoring. On the picket line the horses fidgeted.

At midnight the sentries were changed again, and again at four. This morning no bugler blew reveille. Sentries moved among the men and wakened sergeants, who in turn wakened corporals, who went among the men waking them individually. In the first light of early dawn, the fires were freshened or rebuilt, and breakfast cooked, and after that there was the familiar bustle of a cavalry unit saddling up and preparing to move out. Before the sun was up they fell in silently, and mounted at the command, then executed a left by twos and trailed on north.

Once more Joe Moya rode ahead to scout, and flankers angled away from the main command.

Keefe couldn't help wondering what Burkhalter was thinking about to-day. Was he seeing himself as a general, covered with glory for his successful campaign against the Indians of the plains?

Probably, Keefe thought ruefully. One thing was very sure. Burkhalter did not see himself riding into a Cheyenne trap. He did not see his command slaughtered, decimated, destroyed. He did not see himself pierced with half a dozen arrows, dying in a pool of his own blood in that lonely place. Like everyone else, Keefe supposed, Burkhalter saw in his thoughts only those things he wished to see. And because he did, destruction waited at Rialto Creek.

CHAPTER 14

The day wore on. The ambulances and supply wagons set the pace of the command, slowing it considerably. At times, men had to make crossings over deep arroyos with shovels. In some places, where grades were steep, the wagons had to angle back and forth in a series of switchbacks to reach the top.

They halted at noon by a wide and shallow stream, and the men ate cold rations and refilled their canteens. Each horse was given a morral of oats.

At this halt, Keefe caught Burkhalter watching him, more smouldering anger than usual in his eyes. But Burkhalter did not speak, and after a half-hour rest, the command moved out again.

In mid-afternoon, a trooper rode back to Keefe and saluted him. "Major Burkhalter would like to speak to you, Lieutenant Keefe."

"All right." Keefe glanced at MacPhee, shrugged, then followed the trooper up the line. He reined his horse in beside Major Burkhalter and saluted. "Did you send for me, sir?"

Burkhalter nodded and said harshly, "I want to talk to you. Come with me." He touched spurs to his horse's sides and cantered on ahead. The command maintained its steady pace fifty yards behind. Burkhalter drew his horse in to a walk.

"What did DuBois have to say to you last night?"

Keefe stared at him. He said blankly, "DuBois?" and hoped his face was as innocent as his voice.

Burkhalter replied testily, "Yes, DuBois. There is nothing the matter with your ears, is there, Lieutenant Keefe?"

"No, sir."

"All right then. Tell me what you and DuBois were talking about last night."

Keefe said, "Major, you do not have the right to ask me that."

"Right? Why damn you, I have every right. Everything that affects this command is my responsibility and you damned well know it is."

"I'm not sure that what Lieutenant DuBois had to say to me affects the command."

"You're lying, Keefe. Just as you lied about O'Rourke."

Keefe stared at Burkhalter angrily. His head felt light and he could feel his heart pounding wildly in his chest. He said softly, "Are you trying to provoke me, sir?"

Burkhalter laughed unpleasantly. "You're very righteous-sounding, Keefe. I might have asked the same of you."

"What do you mean, Major?"

"Don't sound so innocent, Lieutenant. I mean my wife. Surely you don't think I'm blind. I saw the very tender way you held her close to you after you so gallantly rescued her from a fate worse than death at the hands of the Indians."

Keefe's face was flaming and the knowledge that it was infuriated him. "You're not suggesting I should have let that Indian kidnap her, are you, Major Burkhalter?"

He knew he was losing this encounter, every round of it.

Burkhalter mimicked sarcastically, "You're not suggesting I should have let that Indian kidnap her, are you, Major Burkhalter?" He glared at Keefe for several moments. "I saw her coming out of your quarters, Lieutenant Keefe. Would you like to explain that to me? Your gall is monumental, sir. I wonder you have not been called out and killed long before this."

Keefe stared straight ahead, so furious he could scarcely control himself. Burkhalter taunted, "Well, Lieutenant?"

Keefe said stonily, "Sir, neither your wife nor I have done anything that requires either explanation or apology. I will not dignify your accusations by denying them."

"You're sounding more righteous all the time, Lieutenant Keefe. Try denying that you came to Fort Kettering for the purpose of revenging yourself against me."

"I do deny it, sir." But Keefe knew that was untrue. He quickly said, "I withdraw that, sir. You're right. I did come here with the idea of revenging myself."

"Ahh. That's better. A little truth might clear the air."

Keefe turned his head and looked squarely into the major's eyes. "Yes, sir. A little truth *might* clear the air. A little truth about what happened at Indian Creek."

Burkhalter stared contemptuously at him. "What good would it do you, Keefe, even if I did tell you what you want to know? Would it restore your father's life? Would it restore his reputation and his rank?"

"It would make me feel better, sir."

"Oh it would, would it? And why should I care how you feel? Do you have so little faith in your own father's word that you need me to bolster it?"

Keefe said, "No, sir, I do not," but even as he said the words he knew they weren't strictly true. He *did* want Burkhalter to admit responsibility for what had happened at Indian Creek.

Burkhalter now probed the weak spot he had found. "You either believe your father or you do not, Lieutenant Keefe. You can't

154

half believe."

"No, sir." Keefe looked squarely at him. "Is that all, sir?"

Burkhalter scowled. "What if I admitted, Lieutenant, that your father told the truth? What if I told you that I *did* attack an hour before the time agreed upon because I wanted the credit for myself?"

"Are you telling me that, sir?"

"Perhaps. There's nothing you can do about it, you know. If you repeat it to anyone, I'll say you're making the whole thing up."

"Yes, sir." Keefe stared straight ahead, not trusting himself to look at Burkhalter. There was elation in him that his father was vindicated, yet there was shame, too, because his vindication had been necessary. He was not proud of himself.

But he realised something else — he was being unnecessarily hard on himself. The whole world had doubted and it was not surprising that he had too. The really important thing now was that a man responsible for literally thousands of unnecessary deaths was boasting about his cleverness. He turned his head and looked at Burkhalter. "There are thousands of men dead because of you, men that need not have died. Because you wanted a general's star. Now it has to be done all over again. When the time comes, Major, you're going to have a lot to answer for."

"Lieutenant, you're being insolent!"

"Yes, sir. But I want to say one thing more. Perhaps no one will completely believe me when I tell them what you have just admitted to me. But it will cloud the issue sufficiently, particularly if things do not turn out too well to-morrow, to keep you from ever regaining that star you want. If that happens, I will have won."

Burkhalter's face was brick-red now. The veins in his forehead stood out prominently. "You damned young pup . . ."

"Is that all, sir?"

"No, God damn you! It isn't all!"

Keefe waited. He had the upper hand momentarily, but he had done himself no favour by gaining it. He had given Burkhalter a more valid reason for hating him and for fearing him. If the major had not been determined to kill him before, he would certainly be determined now. Furthermore, he had a *good* reason now, something he had not had before.

In spite of that, Keefe couldn't resist exploiting the advantage he had gained. He said, "I doubt if I'll have to tell anyone anything, Major, because there's an ambush waiting for us at Rialto Creek. To-morrow night your chances of ever being a general again will be as dead as most of the men in this command."

He glanced at Burkhalter. The major's face had lost colour. It was now pale with icy rage. Burkhalter said, "You're dismissed, Lieutenant. Go back where you belong."

"Yes, sir." Keefe saluted, reined his horse aside, and rode back along the column until he reached the head of L Troop and Captain MacPhee. MacPhee looked strangely at him, but for a moment Keefe would not trust himself to speak.

In spite of what he knew lay ahead of them, in spite of the way he had increased the likelihood that Burkhalter would try to shoot him to-morrow, he felt elated. He now had the means to keep Burkhalter from getting that which he valued above all other things. He had achieved the vengeance for which he had come to Fort Kettering.

He looked at MacPhee. "He admitted it. He admitted that he jumped the gun at Indian Creek and attacked an hour before the appointed time."

MacPhee frowned. "I'm not sure I relish being brought into your dispute with him."

"I'm sorry, Captain. I guess that was unfair."

For several moments they rode in silence. At last MacPhee asked, "What made him admit a thing like that?"

Keefe said, "I don't know. One thing led to another, I guess. He called me up there to ask what DuBois and I were talking about last night."

"You didn't tell him?"

"No, sir."

MacPhee nodded, his expression pre-occupied, and once more that strange bleakness came into his eyes. Watching it steal the life from the captain's expression, Keefe felt coldness creeping into his own chest, felt a like bleakness occupying his own thoughts.

He tried to shake it off, without success. Impatiently, he reined his horse aside and stopped the animal, and watched the troop ride past, each man unconsciously straightening a bit in his saddle as he saw Keefe watching him. When the troop had passed, Keefe touched spurs to his horse and cantered back to the head of it.

The sun sank relentlessly down the western sky. A band of pronghorn antelope stared at the command from the crest of a nearby knoll. A coyote slunk down a dry arroyo as the head of the column neared. Relentlessly they forged north, following the trail upon which Moya had directed them. And among the men, tension mounted steadily.

Sergeant Hochstadt rode behind Lieutenant DuBois and Captain Leighton, eating the dust of the wagons which toiled along ahead of them. In one respect, Hochstadt was like Joe Moya. He missed little either on the land or in the sky. He was not the tracker Moya was, but neither was he blind. Hochstadt had been at Fort Kettering for more than two years now. Prior to that he had served at Fort Laramie. And he was a veteran of the war.

He was a tough, professional soldier, nearing fifty. His skin was like leather, his close-cropped hair turning grey. His eyes were blue, and hard, and surrounded by wrinkles put there by sun and wind.

Hochstadt had a deep distrust for Moya, indeed for all civilian scouts. He knew Moya had lived with the Cheyennes — that was common knowledge at Fort Kettering, and he distrusted any man who could so shift his loyalties at will. A man who would sell out his Cheyenne friends to the Army was as bad as a man who would sell out the Army to his Cheyenne friends.

Scowling, Hochstadt stared at the column

ahead of the wagons. He could see Major Burkhalter riding at the head of B Troop with Sergeant Rounds. He could see MacPhee and Keefe riding at the head of L. He was thinking that there wasn't much that happened, in a post the size of Kettering that did not get around within a day or two. For instance, it was common knowledge that Lieutenant Keefe's father had served with Burkhalter during the war, that he had been forced to resign over an accusation made by Burkhalter concerning the battle of Indian Creek. It was also common knowledge that Burkhalter's wife was interested in Keefe. Hochstadt had little doubt that she had gone out of the post the other night certain that Lieutenant Keefe had seen her and would follow her. Several men had also seen her leave Keefe's quarters brazenly in broad daylight.

Cross-currents like these made Sergeant Hochstadt uneasy. Soldiering ought to be a simple, clear-cut business, uncomplicated by personal animosities and jealousy between the officers. Furthermore, he knew what Lieutenant Keefe claimed O'Rourke had said to him before he died. He also knew Burkhalter had refused to believe Keefe's word.

Hochstadt didn't know what to believe.

Lieutenant Keefe didn't seem the sort to make up things like that even if he did hate Burkhalter for what had happened to his father during the war. And everyone knew Burkhalter was ambitious to be a general again.

He and the other men in the command were simply being used as pawns by their commanding officer, he thought, and the knowledge angered him. Private Shore had died to further Burkhalter's ambition. Others would die to-morrow at dawn. Hochstadt thought it was a lousy cause for which to die.

Still, he was soldier enough to know there was nothing he could do about it. He'd go on following orders just like the rest of the men, just like the officers, for that matter. There was nothing any of them could do. Unless they mutinied, and that would be unthinkable.

In late afternoon, Major Burkhalter called a halt to rest the horses. The men dismounted, loosened cinches, and watered their horses sparingly in a narrow stream. Some unsaddled and fanned their horses' backs with their saddle blankets. A few, not used to long periods in the saddle, cursed the split McClellan saddle with quiet savagery as they rubbed gingerly at their sore buttocks.

Hochstadt managed to ease close to Lieutenant Keefe. He said bluntly, "Some of the men are a bit uneasy, sir — about what O'Rourke said before he died."

"How did you know about that, Hochstadt?"

Hochstadt grinned easily. "It's all over the post, Lieutenant. You reckon Joe Moya is leadin' us into a trap?"

Keefe stiffened slightly, but relaxed under Hochstadt's imperturbable gaze. "That was what O'Rourke's words would seem to indicate. The major does not agree."

"I ain't seen Joe Moya all day. Maybe he's with them red-skinned devils now."

"He's scouting trail, Hochstadt, so we won't have so much trouble getting the wagons through."

"I don't trust that damn' Injun lover, Lieutenant. Stands to reason if he'd sell the Indians out to us, he'd sell us out to them."

"It's not quite the same, Hochstadt. Joe Moya's white."

"Mebbeso, Lieutenant, but was I you, I'd watch him all the same. Them eyes of his, they give me shivers lookin' at them. He'd slit a man's throat fer thirty cents. An' that damn' long hair. He could braid it an' look

162

like any one of them red-skinned murderers."

Keefe said coolly, "All right, Hochstadt. I'll keep an eye on him."

"An' so will I, Lieutenant. So will I." Hochstadt walked back toward the men of his troop, who were watching him.

One asked, "What'd he say, Sarge?"

"Say? About what?"

"About this bein' a trap that damn' Joe Moya set for us."

Hochstadt snorted. "Hell, I wasn't talkin' to him about that. Anyway, this outfit can fight itself out of anything Joe Moya can lead it into and don't you forget it, son."

But he wondered if they could. It was one thing to jump a sleeping village in the dawn. It was quite another to engage an equal or superior number of wide-awake Cheyenne braves unhampered by their women and children. The Cheyennes were fighting men.

But there wasn't a damned thing he could do. His talk with Lieutenant Keefe had told him that, even if the subject hadn't been directly discussed. Burkhalter was in command and they would do what he ordered them to do, no matter what the consequences were to be.

Chapter 15

At irregular intervals, throughout both days, Joe Moya had appeared at the head of the crawling column. Each time he would ride along with Major Burkhalter for half a mile or so while he pointed out the most practicable route in the land ahead. He would say, "Follow this drainage, Major, an' about five or six miles up there you'll come to a deep, wooded ravine. Skirt it for a mile, an' then drop off down a long shallow draw toward the northwest."

He would ride off, trotting his horse, and disappear again into the land ahead. No one ever saw Joe Moya ride along the crest of a ridge. No one ever saw Joe Moya unless he wanted to be seen. He knew all the tricks an Indian knows about travelling through this land, showing neither himself nor any trail of dust.

He was busy and working hard, not only to guide the column along trails easy for their wagons to negotiate, but also along trails which did not cross those of travelling Cheyenne war parties heading for the village at Rialto Creek.

He found several of these trails, and each time made a head count as best he could. The total mounted steadily in his mind. If his estimate was anywhere near right, and he thought it was, there were going to be between seven hundred and a thousand Cheyennes waiting for Burkhalter's command at Rialto Creek.

His face was sombre as he rode, filled with the bleakness of his loss, with the emptiness of the years ahead. But growing now in his eyes was a certain fierce exuberance because every mile brought Major Burkhalter's command closer to its doom. Red Earth Woman would be avenged. By this time to-morrow, Red Earth Woman and the children would be avenged.

Moya was aware of the doubts the troopers had concerning him. He could see it in the hard, distrustful way they looked at him. But he also knew how helpless they were to change anything. Burkhalter was in command and Burkhalter had closed his mind to any doubts he might have entertained. Burkhalter wanted to annihilate the village on Rialto Creek. It had become an obsession with him. He wanted it so badly he had convinced himself it was going to be as easy as the village on Cut Nose Creek had been.

In late afternoon, Moya rode his scrambling horse up the steep, shaly slope of a flat-topped butte. He halted the animal beneath the twelve-foot rim and tied him behind a twisted cedar growing there. He climbed the rim with little difficulty and crawled out on top, staying prone, staring across the undulating plain.

From here he could see the drainage of Rialto Creek, winding away toward the north and east, still a dozen miles away. He could see the rough, badlands-type country east of it. He smoothed a place on the ground before him and deliberately traced Rialto Creek with a forefinger, making a dot where he had told Tall Elk to locate the village that was to be the bait.

Now, he marked off the badlands east of Rialto Creek by making a series of crosses in the dust. Coming back, he marked this escarpment with a semicircle, then showed the trail of the command with a lightly traced line, ending with an X to show where they would camp to-night.

With this done, he marked an "N" where north was on his map. Thoughtfully, afterward, he stared out across the plain again. From this elevation, he could see almost thirty miles. It was an empty land that met his gaze — empty to a hastily scanning eye at least. But there were things to be seen out there, if the eye was trained and the vision sharp. A scattering of minute black dots straight east was a small herd of buffalo. A wisp that seemed almost to be imagination was the lifting of dust from a small whirlwind. That tiny dot, all of fifteen miles away, which had just appeared, was a column of Cheyennes emerging from a dry wash that had previously hidden them.

Motionless, he remained for half an hour, patiently scanning the plain. Closer, he picked up another group of Cheyennes, only three this time. He saw a lone buck antelope standing on a knoll. He saw a badger waddle along at the foot of the shale slope that dropped away from the rimrock of this butte. He saw a mouse scurrying among the rocks not a dozen yards from his horse, and a sand lizard closer still.

Satisfied at last, he crawled back down over the rim. He untied his horse, mounted, and slid him down the slope. He turned back toward the south and lifted the animal to an easy lope, making no effort now to conceal himself. An hour later he reached the troops, halted, and turned his horse in beside Major Burkhalter. He said, "Camp in an hour, Major. It'll be a dry camp and no fires. The village we're after will be about ten miles farther on. We don't dare camp any closer'n that."

Burkhalter nodded. "How well do you

know the land around that village, Joe?"

"Like the back of my hand. I can draw it out for you."

"Good." Burkhalter's face had a tight, anxious set to it. His eyes were narrowed slightly, his mouth firm. His body was almost rigid, and very tense.

Moya thought, "You son-of-a-bitch, I hope you die real slow. I hope you get it in the gut and have to lay there hurtin' whilst you watch your command cut to bits."

Burkhalter glanced at him and Moya looked quickly away, afraid his eyes might give his thoughts away. But Burkhalter did not really seem to notice him. Burkhalter's thoughts were on the battle. Even more they were on the future, on the recommendation he hoped to receive, on the brigadier general's star he now figured was a certainty.

Moya let his head sink forward onto his chest. He closed his eyes. He drowsed, and the column plodded patiently on. The sun continued to dip toward the western plain and toward the mountains, hidden behind a hundred or more miles of mist and surface haze.

Moya seemed to drowse, yet if his body seemed relaxed, his spirit was tense as any fiddle string, his mind alert. There must be no slip-ups now. Not with Burkhalter come this far. Not with the Cheyennes waiting to ambush him. To-night he'd leave as soon as it was dark, ostensibly to scout the village. He'd go into their camps and he'd talk to Tall Elk and to the other chiefs. He wanted no mistakes, no reckless, ill-considered actions taken by any of the younger braves. It was a carefully planned ambush and ought to go off like one.

The butte he had climbed to scan the plain seemed to rise up out of the land ahead as they approached. The sun dropped like a flaming ball of molten gold into the sagebrush-covered plain. The grey, the cool of dusk came down.

In this light they camped, almost in the shadow of the butte. They ate cold rations, hardtack, and dried apples and drank cold water from the barrels lashed to the sides of the supply wagons. They fed their horses grain and tied them to the picket line.

By a lantern's light inside one of the wagons, Moya took pencil and paper and drew his map for the major and his officers. He drew it carefully as he had drawn it in the dust of the butte top, and he marked the mileages off on it. Then he withdrew. He headed toward his horse, tied on the picket line.

A moment later, Lieutenant Keefe

dropped from the wagon. He stood for a moment, peering into the darkness. Hearing a stir and the murmur of voices from the direction of the picket line, he hurried that way, arriving just as Moya was riding out, heading towards the north.

Swiftly he saddled a horse, the nearest horse, using the first saddle he encountered in the dark. Mounting swiftly, he turned the horse's head north toward the direction in which Moya had just disappeared. He was filled with doubts and suddenly scared, riding off alone in the dark like this. But he had to know where Joe Moya was going and what he meant to do. The lives of all the men in this command might depend on what he was able to find out to-night.

Back inside the wagon, under the canvas, their faces lighted eerily by the single guttering lamp, the officers stared at Major Burkhalter warily. Burkhalter jabbed at the map with a stubby forefinger. He glanced up, saying, "Now, by God, let's get down to the business of this thing." He let his eyes drift from one face to another and when he had looked at all of them said irritably, "Now where the hell did that goddam Keefe disappear to?"

"He dropped out of the wagon right after

Moya did. I figured he'd be right back." This was Captain MacPhee, who knew by now that Keefe would not be back. Keefe intended to try following the scout.

Burkhalter said, "Never mind. Look at this map, all of you." He smoothed it on the wagon floor. He traced a route from their present camp to a spot just below the village, which Moya had marked with a cross. "I will take what there is of B Troop, and Captain Leighton and DuBois with K. We'll circle up behind the village, between it and this area that Moya has indicated as badlands. He says there is a prominent ridge behind the village."

Nobody spoke. After a moment Burkhalter went on, "MacPhee and Keefe will take L Troop and advance along the bed of Rialto Creek until they are about a hundred yards short of the village edge. MacPhee, I want you to stay put until you hear our gunfire. Then you are to advance at a gallop and destroy whatever Indians try to escape along the bed of the stream."

MacPhee glanced up. "Are we to remain mounted or dismount and fight on foot?"

"That will be up to your own discretion, Captain. It will depend, I suppose, on how quickly the Indians pull themselves together."

"Yes, sir."

"This plan worked like clockwork at Cut Nose Creek and there is no reason to believe it will not work equally well here. Are there any questions, gentlemen?"

MacPhee said, "I presume you're relying on the intelligence that Moya supplied, Major. That there would be sixty to eighty warriors in this village we are going to attack?"

"I am."

"And what if O'Rourke's story of an ambush is correct?"

Burkhalter exploded. "Goddam it, Captain MacPhee, who is in command here, you or me? If I hear any more of that nonsense I swear I'll bring charges against you for insubordination!"

"Things like that won't matter if we are all dead, will they, Major Burkhalter?" MacPhee's voice betrayed his fury, for all that it was icy cold and calm.

"Are you afraid of these savages, Captain? Are you afraid of the action we expect to see to-morrow? Perhaps the charge I bring against you ought to be one of cowardice."

For a long time there was a dead silence inside the wagon. The lamp flickered, casting a shifting yellow light on the faces of these men. When MacPhee's voice finally

172

came, it was almost inaudible. "When this battle is over with, Burkhalter, you will answer to me personally for that!"

Burkhalter's voice was taunting. "My pleasure, Captain."

Again there was silence, the cold silence of disapproval from Burkhalter's officers, an almost contemptuous silence from the major himself. At last he said, "Dismissed. Get some sleep. Reveille will be at three and we'll move out at three-thirty. That ought to put us at the village by the time it's light enough to shoot."

They crawled stiffly out of the wagon and the major blew out the lamp. In silence they groped their way to where their beds had been laid, inside the circle formed by the wagons which had, when they halted, been drawn into a circle as a precautionary measure.

Since the major was within hearing range, there was no talking, not even any grumbling. Raging with helpless anger, MacPhee lay staring at the stars.

He heard the sentries' soft calls, giving the numbers of their posts and the information that all was well. He heard the slight commotion later when the sentries were relieved.

He was remembering things that were

over with, his mind making the long journey back across the years. He was seeing himself as a plebe at West Point, and as a graduate, and he was seeing Molly the way she'd been during that short year they'd had before she died. He was feeling again the exquisite pain of losing her, and the bleak hopelessness that had possessed him afterward.

Fifteen years had passed between her death and the outbreak of the war, and sometimes it almost seemed as though those years had never been. Then the war had broken out, and for a long time it seemed as if the Union was going to lose. He'd met Sarah that first year of the war, and should have married her, he realised now. It had been cowardly of him not to marry her but he'd been afraid — of experiencing that nearly unbearable pain of loss again. Eventually she'd married someone else and he had gone his way alone.

Alone as he was to-night. Alone as he would be to-morrow when the battle with the Cheyennes began.

He would live out the remaining hours of his life alone, and to-morrow he would die alone. Of that he was very sure. And there would be nothing left behind, nothing to show that he had ever been here on earth.

CHAPTER 16

For a little while, Keefe tried to catch up with Moya sufficiently to enable him to follow the trail-wise scout. He had gone no more than a mile before good sense told him it was impossible. The night was nearly completely black, the only light being that from the stars, filtered through a thin overcast. If he got close enough to Moya to follow him, Moya would know it and his chance of learning anything would be gone if, indeed, Moya did not try to kill him outright and afterward blame it on the Indians.

So he slowed his horse and angled east with the deliberate intention of avoiding Moya should the man for any reason stop. There was very little chance of his being able to learn anything conclusive out here in the dark but he had to try. The lives of more than two hundred men depended on it.

Alone now in this empty land, he rode with extreme care even though he knew how unlikely it was that any Indians would be prowling around this late. If O'Rourke had been right, and Keefe thought he had, the Indians would be in their camps, planning their own strategy against an enemy about to walk foolishly into their baited trap.

Fortunately, Keefe's horse was better able to see than he, and picked a surefooted, steady way through the blackness of the night. Occasionally sagebrush brushed against Keefe's legs or feet. Occasionally the horse seemed to drop unexpectedly out from under him as the animal slid down a steep embankment into a wash.

The way Moya had drawn for Burkhalter and his officers in the flickering light inside the wagon seemed burned indelibly on his brain. He could see it even now, and the directions on it, the big, scrawled N which indicated north. He glanced up at the sky several times, orienting himself by the stars.

Ten miles, it was, to the Indian village on Rialto Creek. Ten miles. And east of the village was rough country resembling a badlands. At least that was what Moya had said. Whether even that much of the scout's story was true or not, Keefe didn't know. Probably there *was* a badlands and probably the hidden force with which the Cheyennes intended to annihilate the troopers was concealed in it.

Keefe had gone more than eight miles, he guessed, when his horse stopped suddenly. No amount of urging would make the horse go on. Keefe dismounted and inched himself forward cautiously.

A cold breeze struck him in the face, cold blowing up out of a canyon immediately ahead. He had reached the badlands rim. Thank God his horse could see better in the dark than he.

He backed off and remounted his horse. Reining left, he allowed the horse to follow the badlands rim. Now and again the horse would balk again. Each time Keefe would allow him to change direction sufficiently to avoid the precipice.

This way, he travelled another mile, his uneasiness growing all the time. The horse was noisy, stepping sometimes on twigs, blundering sometimes into clumps of brush or scrubby thorn trees. Several times, Keefe glanced up at the sky. The overcast was thinning but even if it cleared entirely he still would not have enough light to see.

A glow in the east, however, announced the rising of the moon. He decided to wait for that.

He dismounted and tied his horse to a gnarled cedar tree. He moved off a ways and sat down to wait. He wondered where Moya was.

Slowly the glow in the east strengthened and at last the moon poked its rim above the plain.

Its outline was blurred because of the overcast, but it cast enough light upon the land to see the ground, to see clumps of brush and cedar trees and, most important of all, to see the yawning blackness of the canyon in sharp contrast to the lighter land along the rim.

Leaving his horse, Keefe began to move stealthily along the badlands rim. It was unavoidable that he sometimes dislodged a rock. It was inevitable that he sometimes snapped a twig. Once he heard a large animal, probably a deer, plunge away from him, making a thunderous crashing in the brush.

His revolver was now in his hand although he knew if he used it he might bring the savages down upon him. He stood still and silent for a long time after the crashing died away, smiling ruefully at his own startled fright.

His smile faded. His head turned slightly, listening. His eyes narrowed, trying to pierce the darkness ahead of him. There was a blur of something there, blacker than the rest of this night landscape . . .

How long he stayed frozen thus, he could not have said. It seemed like an eternity. He was conscious of time slipping away from him and knew if he did not get on with it, he might be caught out here by the coming of dawn, accused by Burkhalter of desertion in the face of the enemy and God knew what else. And then that blur of blackness moved . . .

It moved and became the crouched, tense form of a Cheyenne brave. It came toward him, closer, closer . . .

Keefe stopped breathing. How many more were there in the shadows surrounding him? If he attacked this one, how many others would attack him in turn? Should he let the Indian go past, or should he attack?

He never knew how he would have decided had the decision been left up to him. It was not. The Indian came straight toward him along a course that would bring them within a yard of each other, a collision course . . .

While the brave was yet six feet away, Keefe moved suddenly. His right arm raised the revolver like a club. He sprang forward, closing with the brave, bringing down the upraised gun . . .

The smell of the Cheyenne was rank in his nostrils even before they touched, a smell compounded of sweat, and leather, and campfire smoke, and the grease of animals, the smell of horse, and a wild smell upon which no man could put a name. The clubbed gun slammed against the Cheyenne, grazing his head and coming down on his shoulder with stunning force.

The Indian grunted gustily, a sound made up both of surprise and pain. Then his hand, holding a knife withdrawn like lightning from a sheath at his belt, slashed savagely at Keefe.

The blade struck the metal buckle of his belt and was deflected. Even so it cut through tunic and underwear and flesh beneath, bringing a quick, warm rush of blood. Keefe groped for and seized the Indian's wrist with his free left hand, in the meantime raising the gun again.

But the Indian caught his right wrist, trying to twist it, trying to force him to drop the gun. This way they stood, braced, straining against each other, pitting brute strength against brute strength, with death the price to be paid by whoever first was forced to yield.

Blood pounded in Keefe's head like the monotonous, throbbing sound of a drum. His breath came from between clenched teeth. He could feel his muscles weakening. He was young and he was strong but he knew he was no match in raw endurance for this sinewy young Cheyenne brave.

He would not be able to raise his gun with

the Cheyenne holding so fiercely on to his wrist. Nor would he be able to match the Cheyenne in keeping the knife from his body. Soon now his strength would become like water and the knife would bury itself. His life would pour out of the hole it made . . .

A calculated risk. He had to take the calculated risk. He had to save his life in any way he could and that meant firing the gun.

Nor was there time to consider the step he now was forced to take. There was only time to take it, quickly, before it would be too late.

Keefe thumbed the hammer back, exerted the last, spasmodic burst of strength remaining in his right arm and shoved the gun barrel against the belly of the young Cheyenne. His forefinger tightened and there was a muffled report, a violent recoil from the gun, and the blinding, choking cloud of acrid powder smoke.

He held, then, fiercely, frantically, savagely, to the Cheyenne's right wrist. He held and prayed silently that the Indian's strength would ebb before his did.

Breath exploded from the Cheyenne's lungs. The strength of his hand, gripping Keefe's wrist, relaxed and it fell away. His body slumped and Keefe let it fall, crumpled and inert, to the ground at his feet. He stepped back warily, the gun ready in his hand, thumb on hammer, prepared for a second shot and a third.

His ears searched the darkness for a sound. His eyes probed it for a movement, for shape. Only silence met his ears. Only darkness and stillness met his eyes.

Without sheathing the revolver, he stooped and took the knife from the Indian's hand. Knife in one hand, revolver in the other, he now moved on in the direction he had been going before he encountered the Indian.

More than ever before, he knew he had to go on. The Indian's presence proved that O'Rourke had told the truth. It proved the trap as nothing else ever could. Had the village on Rialto Creek been asleep, as Major Burkhalter believed, there would have been no Indian sentry here.

It proved something else to Keefe, that there were other Indian guards. He was still in deadly danger and would remain so until he had retreated and headed back toward the bivouac.

Cautiously he crept along, keeping close to the canyon rim where brush grew higher than it did farther away from it, trying to watch both the ground and the land surrounding him. His teeth had begun to chatter slightly, both from the night's chill and from the tension and uncertainty. He clenched them angrily.

Almost reluctantly, he holstered the gun and transferred the Indian's knife to his right hand. Faintly he heard a dog barking up ahead. Faintly he heard a pack of coyotes yammering somewhere in the badlands on his right.

Suddenly he froze. A voice had reached him, a human voice, and now he heard another making reply to it. He could not understand the words, nor even tell if they had been spoken in English or Cheyenne, but he halted and waited there motionless, scarcely daring to breathe until he heard one of the voices speak again. This time he carefully marked the direction from which the sound had come.

Directly ahead of him, they were, barring the way he knew he had to go. He'd have to circle, giving them a wide enough berth so that they wouldn't hear him even if he was unfortunate enough to snap a twig or stir a rock.

Carefully, he sat down, placing the knife on the ground at his side. Carefully, he removed his boots. He got to his feet again and, carrying the boots in his left hand, the knife in his right, began making a wide circle to his left.

Prior to each step, he felt the ground ahead with a foot before putting his weight on it. He avoided clumps of brush, aware that even the sound of a branch rubbing against his pants might alert the sentries he had heard. With a part of his mind, he counted the steps he took. Ten. Twenty. Thirty. Now he turned slightly toward the north and went on, scarcely daring to breathe, the knife hilt clutched so hard that his knuckles were white, his palm slick with sweat.

The distant dog barked again, to be answered by another one. He hoped he would encounter no dogs prowling around this far out.

The Cheyenne sentries were behind him now, the village straight ahead. When he thought he was far enough past the pair, he sat down carefully once more and replaced his boots. He'd need them if he had to run, would need them if he had to fight.

He reached the edge of the shallow ridge upon which he was travelling, and suddenly the village on Rialto Creek was ahead, spread out on the long slope that dropped away from this ridge to the creek.

Fires were burning down below, and

Indians sitting around the fires. Other Indians were moving back and forth along the village streets. Keefe saw no squaws, though he knew how difficult it would be to tell the difference this far away, and he saw no children. All those he saw looked like men to him.

That was enough to satisfy him that he was right, that O'Rourke also had been right. But he knew it would not satisfy Burkhalter. He had to have more.

He squatted silently on the ground, staring at the village below and ahead of him. Occasionally he would look carefully behind, and always his ears were tuned to each small sound. He knew he was in over his depth doing this. He was no frontier scout; he was no Indian. His senses were not sharpened and honed by danger as theirs were. He could only do his best, relying on his experience conducting wartime patrols to get him through.

He stayed there quietly for a long time, wondering what kind of proof he could get that would satisfy Major Burkhalter. Perhaps if he could locate the force the Indians had hidden in the badlands . . .

He started to get up but sank back suddenly as he saw forms begin to emerge from one of the hide lodges down below. The first two men out were Indians, but the third . . .

The third was Joe Moya, Burkhalter's scout. Keefe narrowed his eyes with sudden anger as he watched.

Moya turned when the Indians were outside the lodge. He seemed to be speaking to them all. Then he walked behind the lodge. A moment later he emerged again, this time mounted on his horse. He raised a hand to the group of Indians and rode off in the direction of the cavalry bivouac ten miles away.

Keefe let a long slow breath escape his lungs. He had what he needed now. Once Burkhalter knew Moya had been in the Indian camp he would be forced to admit that he had blundered into a trap. Perhaps it would be impossible for him to extricate his command from all danger at this late date. But at least he wouldn't walk into it blind to-morrow. He could attempt an orderly retreat and force the Indians to fight on his terms instead of theirs.

Keefe turned his head and studied the land around him for a long time before he moved. Then he got deliberately to his feet. He needn't worry about encountering Moya going back. Moya would be far ahead. All he needed to worry about were the two

Cheyenne guards between him and his horse.

Making a wider circle around them this time, he moved carefully back in the direction he had come. Every nerve, every instinct told him how urgent it was that he get back quickly to the command. Time was running out for them. Time would have completely run out if he did not get back in time to stop their attack on the village waiting on Rialto Creek for them.

But even as every instinct screamed for him to hurry, caution told him that if he was not careful he would not get back at all. He had no assurance the Indians he had encountered were the only ones doing sentry duty out here in the dark. There might be others. He might blunder into one at any time.

It seemed an eternity to Keefe, that distance between the ridge top where he had halted and the place where he had tied his horse. But he reached his horse at last, untied the animal, and swung astride. He drummed his heels against the horse's sides and the long-legged cavalry remount broke into a gallop and then into a steady run. Keefe let the reins go loose, allowing the horse to pick his own path across the brush-covered plain.

CHAPTER 17

Never had ten miles seemed longer to Keefe than tonight. He knew he covered it in a little more than an hour, but it seemed like ten.

He arrived at the bivouac an hour before reveille and rode in openly, not wanting to risk trying to get in without being observed. The sentries would be nervous and trigger happy and would shoot at anything. He was still a hundred yards out when the familiar challenge rang out, "Halt! Who goes there?"

He smiled faintly to himself. Regulations dictated the form of the challenge but it was a little ridiculous when Indians were all around. He called back promptly, "Lieutenant Keefe."

"Advance and be recognised."

He rode forward slowly. The sentry looked up, recognised him, and said, "I didn't know you were out there, sir."

Keefe didn't reply. He rode on in and dismounted just outside the small circle formed by the wagons. He tied his exhausted horse to one of the wagons and strode into the circle.

Burkhalter was awake, sitting up in his bed. "Just where the hell do you think you've been, Keefe?" His voice was harsh and he made no effort to keep it low. The other officers stirred and MacPhee sat up. "What the hell? What's going on?"

Burkhalter's voice was sarcastic. "Your goddamned new lieutenant has been out riding around the countryside. Did you enjoy yourself, Lieutenant Keefe?"

"Sir, I have a report to make."

"Oh you do, do you? Damn you, I ought to put you under arrest. Who the hell gave you permission to leave this camp?"

"Sir, I scouted the Indian village and . . ."

"You what?" Burkhalter's voice was an incredulous roar.

"I scouted the Indian village, sir. I saw Moya ride out and I wanted to see what he was up to so . . ."

Burkhalter began to curse savagely. Keefe said stubbornly, "Sir, I have a report to make. Moya was in that Indian village talking to the Cheyennes. I saw him. I saw him with my own two eyes."

"You what?" Burkhalter's voice seemed almost out of control. The man was up now. Moonlight touched his hair, which was tousled and standing straight on end. He was hunched forward slightly as though at any moment he would attack his subordinate.

"I saw Moya, Major. Inside the village

talking to the Indians."

Burkhalter turned to MacPhee. "Place this man under arrest, Captain! I want him held under a two-man guard until this action is over with!"

"Hadn't you ought to hear what he has to say, Major? I think . . ."

"I don't give a goddam what you think! I've heard enough from him and I've heard enough from you, MacPhee! I don't know what his game is, but he's a liar and I won't have him in my command! Is that clear to you?"

"It's clear, Major. But I think you're wrong. I think you ought to call Moya over here and see what he has to say for himself."

From the darkness a voice asked, "Did I hear my name?" Moya walked into the little clearing from out of the shadows. Keefe could hear the whole camp stirring now. All the officers here were sitting up. Some were getting their boots pulled on. Moya said, "What is it you want to know from me, Captain MacPhee?"

"Keefe says he saw you in the Cheyenne camp, talking to the Indians."

Moya chuckled softly. Keefe wished desperately that he could see Moya's face, and that Burkhalter could see it too. But in the moonlight, with his face in shadow, the scout wasn't going to give anything away.

Moya said reluctantly, "Major, I don't like giving the lie to one of your officers. Maybe he saw someone he thought looked like me, an Indian with some white man's clothes . . . I don't know. But he didn't see me, Major. If I went into that damned village I wouldn't get out of it again."

For a long moment there was silence. At last Burkhalter said triumphantly, "Are you satisfied, MacPhee?"

"Not exactly, sir. I don't think you're justified in putting Lieutenant Keefe under arrest. I think it would be wiser to send out a patrol. A lot more is involved here than whether Lieutenant Keefe saw Moya with the Indians or whether he lied about it or made a mistake. There is still a question in my mind as to what O'Rourke meant . . ."

"Captain MacPhee!" Burkhalter's voice was a choked roar.

MacPhee was silent.

Burkhalter's words were now measured and deliberately cold. "You will carry out my order and put Lieutenant Keefe under arrest. You will put a two-man guard over him and leave him here with the wagons when we ride out."

"Yes, sir."

Burkhalter walked to where Keefe stood.

"Give me your revolver, Lieutenant."

Keefe handed over his revolver, butt first. Burkhalter took it and handed it to MacPhee. He turned to look at Keefe again. "I intend to see to it that you get a general court-martial, Keefe. I intend to break you for this!"

Keefe said softly, "The way you broke my father, sir?"

MacPhee interrupted before Burkhalter could explode. "Come along, Keefe." He seized Keefe's arm and literally dragged him away. He pulled him angrily between two wagons. On the other side he said furiously, "Damn it, Keefe, have you lost your mind?"

"No, but he has, Captain. He's taking this command into a trap. You'll be lucky if you all aren't killed."

"I'm beginning to think he's right. I'm beginning to think you are making the whole thing up!"

Keefe walked to his horse and removed the Indian's knife from his saddlebag. He handed it to MacPhee. "I didn't make this up, Captain."

MacPhee took the knife and looked at it. Keefe said, "I killed an Indian to-night, Captain. That's his knife. He was standing guard more than a mile from the village." He realised suddenly that the mere fact of the Indian being on sentry duty proved nothing — except perhaps that the village on Rialto Creek didn't intend to share the fate of the one on Cut Nose Creek.

MacPhee asked, "Did you see any Indians other than those in the village?"

Keefe shook his head. "But I'm sure they're there. They're in the badlands, Captain, and when they hear shooting they'll come boiling out."

MacPhee said, "I'm sorry, Keefe. You haven't convinced me. How can you be sure it was Moya you saw in that village talking to the Indians? How far away were you?"

"A quarter mile."

"And the only light was that from the fires and the moon. You could have made a mistake."

"I could, but I didn't, Captain."

MacPhee said reluctantly, "I'm sorry about this, Keefe." He yelled into the darkness, "Corporal of the guard!"

Several moments of silence passed. At last a trooper approached and saluted. MacPhee said, "Lieutenant Keefe has been placed under arrest. Detail two men as a guard for him."

"Yes, sir." The corporal's voice was shocked, and Keefe suddenly realised the man was Corporal Ord.

MacPhee repeated, "I'm sorry, Keefe," and walked away, disappearing between two wagons.

Corporal Ord stared at Keefe embarrassedly. Keefe said, "Corporal, I will stay right here."

"Yes, sir. Thank you, sir." Ord hurried away.

The overcast had thinned and the moon was now very bright. After a few moments two men approached Keefe and saluted him. They seemed as embarrassed as Ord had been. One of them said, "We're supposed to guard you, sir."

Keefe smiled faintly. He fished a cigar from his pocket, lighted it, then sat down on the ground with his back to a wagon wheel. The two troopers stood at attention uncomfortably, facing him.

The camp began to waken. Men went around waking the few still sleeping troopers. Cold rations were distributed.

Silent troopers sought the picket line, found their horses, and saddled them. At last Burkhalter called "Fall in," and when the line had formed, called, "Count off!"

The count went down the line. "One, two. One, two." When it had reached the other end, Burkhalter shouted, "Prepare to mount . . . mount! Right by twos . . . ho-o-o!" Guides and guidon bearers led the troops out of the bivouac area. The wagons remained, circled, grey in the cold light of the half-moon overhead. On the picket line remained the mules that had drawn them, and the horses of the few troopers who would stay behind as wagon guards, and as guards for Lieutenant Keefe.

Keefe, standing now, watched them ride away and disappear into the cold glow of moonlight that lay across the plain. There was already the faintest of grey lines along the horizon in the east. It had been timed just right, he thought. By the time it was light enough to shoot, the command would be waiting on the ridge behind the village on Rialto Creek.

And he would be here, deprived of the action, deprived of the right to share whatever fate awaited them. He cursed softly, angrily, to himself.

The sounds of the departing column faded and disappeared. Keefe began to pace nervously back and forth, occasionally glancing at the greying horizon in the east. The command would be slaughtered, he thought with bleak hopelessness. If O'Rourke had been right and if he himself was right, there could be a thousand Indians waiting for Burkhalter to ride into their trap.

The tempo of his pacing increased. The two troopers stared nervously at him.

The command had been gone less than fifteen minutes when Keefe heard the drum of hard-pounding hooves. He stared in the direction they had gone. The guards brought their carbines up to a ready position but lowered them again self-consciously as Captain MacPhee rode his plunging horse into camp. MacPhee said, "Get a horse, Keefe." He looked at the two guards. "Get your horses, I'll take the responsibility for releasing Lieutenant Keefe."

"Yes, sir!" Both men seemed relieved. They ran toward the horses on the picket line, with Keefe following.

MacPhee led out at a steady gallop. Keefe rode close behind and the two troopers rode close at his horse's heels. A mile or so out, MacPhee slowed enough to hand Keefe his revolver. Keefe shoved it into the holster at his side.

In silence, afterward, they continued, holding the same steady pace. Half an hour passed before they brought the rear of the column into sight. MacPhee slowed his horse and called to Keefe. "Stay at the rear of the troop, Keefe. There's no use tangling with him now. Time enough for that when the battle's over with."

Keefe nodded shortly even though he knew MacPhee no longer was looking at him. He watched the captain ride on ahead.

L Troop was bringing up the rear to-day since L Troop had been designated by Major Burkhalter as the force that would move up the bed of Rialto Creek and cut off possible escape by hostiles after the initial attack had been made by B and K.

He let his horse canter along at the extreme rear of the column. The two enlisted men that had been assigned as guards fell in behind.

The sky in the east was now plainly grey. The band of grey widened steadily but it was still too dark to shoot. Keefe found himself wondering what was going to happen to them to-day. He wondered if he had, indeed, been wrong, if he had imagined what O'Rourke had said. He smiled ruefully at his thoughts. Tell a man often enough that he is wrong and he begins to doubt himself.

He sincerely hoped he had been wrong. He hoped the Indians in the village were the only Indians for a hundred miles. And for a little while he almost had himself believing it was true.

Burkhalter slowed the column to a trot, held them at it for almost a mile, then lifted them to a gallop again. They dropped down a long rise and entered the bed of a creek, Rialto Creek, Keefe supposed, and they travelled in the creek bed for another mile. Then Burkhalter halted the column with a raised hand, with no audible command.

Keefe hung back, nearly hidden by brush and trees. He saw Burkhalter beckon to his officers and saw them hold a hasty council of war in the cold grey light of early dawn.

It was peaceful here. The creek tumbled along, sometimes over flat rocks, making a slight rushing sound, sometimes smoothing out and deepening. Keefe wondered idly if there were trout in it.

Small birds, disturbed by the column of grim-faced cavalrymen, chirped gleefully. A man coughed, covering his mouth with his hand. Saddle leathers squeaked, and occasionally stirrups clanged against other stirrups.

He'd been wrong about one thing, thought Keefe. Burkhalter had apparently not planned to kill him during the heat of battle, else he would not have detached him and left him behind.

Burkhalter's voice droned on. At last he dismissed the officers and they returned to their respective commands. Burkhalter raised himself in his stirrups and waved an arm. B Troop and K moved out, leaving the creek bottom, climbing out and heading up the long ridge behind the Indian camp.

Keefe's breath sighed slowly out as he watched them go. He realised that his whole body was tense. Perhaps, he thought, Burkhalter *had* originally intended to kill him during the battle here. Previous indications certainly had been that he did. Even MacPhee had warned him about it. But his leaving camp last night had changed Burkhalter's mind. Killing was risky even in the heat of battle, particularly when the intended victim is on guard. Discrediting carries no risk with it at all. Left behind, Keefe would have been discredited no matter what happened here to-day. Court-martialled and stripped of his rank, he might even have been accused of cowardice, of making the whole thing up about scouting the Indian village during the night.

He spurred his horse and rode to the head of the column. MacPhee was watching him, uncertainty in his eyes as though he was trying to decide what this command would face when the battle began. He said, "Burkhalter said to wait until we heard their shots. Then we are to charge up the bottom of the creek."

Keefe looked straight at him, holding the

199

captain's glance with his own steady one. He said, "Captain, everything I have said is the gospel truth. I'm absolutely certain that there are close to a thousand Indians up there ahead of us."

His words carried to the nearest troopers in the column and suddenly their eyes were scared, their faces whiter than they had been before. The silence ran on, and on, until it seemed nothing would ever make it end.

But end it did. Sounding like strings of firecrackers on the Fourth of July, the guns of Major Burkhalter's command popped along the shallow ridge, rolling down the gentle slope to the ears of the men waiting in the bed of Rialto Creek. MacPhee raised an arm, and waved it forward, and L Troop surged into motion, the men now standing in their stirrups and letting go with a long-drawn-out battle cry.

CHAPTER 18

Along here, both sides of the creek were lined with brush and trees. Beyond, on the right, the land raised steeply by half a dozen feet to level ground before beginning its gradual rise to the crest of the ridge. Because of the impediment of brush and trees, MacPhee kept his column in the water shallows where the hooves of their galloping horses sent up a great flying spray.

Keefe's revolver was in his hand. Beside him galloped the guidon bearer, and slightly ahead of him the captain rode. MacPhee had drawn his sabre and now held it above his head.

The sounds of L Troop galloping all but drowned out the sounds of firing from the ridge. But they were getting closer now, closer to the firing, which seemed, if anything, to have intensified.

Then, without warning, they burst out of the tree-lined creek bottom into the open, and the village lay there on the sloping stream bank before them. Beyond was the long slope of the ridge and B and K Troops spread along the slope in a line, galloping straight down it toward the village edge.

They were firing as they came, standing in their stirrups, yelling. Some of the noncoms were waving sabres instead of guns, the sun catching the flashing steel and reflecting from it brilliantly. The smell of powder smoke was in the air. A blue cloud of it rolled along the ridge on the light early morning breeze. The birds were still . . .

MacPhee and Keefe rode on to the far edge of the village so that the rest of L Troop could get out of the trees and be effective against the Indians. As he rode, Keefe saw that he had, indeed, been right. This was no sleeping village, caught by surprise and easy to slaughter and destroy. Men erupted from its tipis, armed men. They fired with steady precision at Burkhalter's force galloping down the slope. Others faced toward Rialto Creek, waiting calmly until the men of L Troop would turn toward them and thus present steadier targets for their guns.

The last of L Troop splashed out of the trees, and MacPhee let his long command roll back, "Right by twos . . . ho-o-o-o! Charge!" He spurred his horse up the tapering bank toward the village, riding a dozen yards ahead of the undulating line of mounted cavalrymen. They were going to fight through the village mounted, Keefe realised. It was a risky manœuvre during which there was some danger of L Troop's bullets killing the men of B and K Troops, and vice versa. But MacPhee had seen the steadiness with which the Indians were facing Burkhalter's charge. He was risking everything trying to break their ranks and put them to flight.

Keefe's horse had come out of the water and now took the steep, tapering bank in a couple of lunges, a length behind MacPhee's wildly galloping mount. Keefe's glance raised to the ridge behind Burkhalter's galloping men.

He almost froze with shock. He knew it was a sight he would never forget, not as long as he lived.

Rank upon rank of mounted, painted Cheyennes flowed over the crest of that ridge like some barbaric tide. Ten ranks, a dozen ranks deep they came, warbonnets fluttering in the breeze, rifles and lances raised. They came silently until the whole savage horde was visible, and then a chorus of their shrill, fierce, bloodthirsty cries tore through the morning air.

Burkhalter's men stopped as though they had run into a wall. His troopers jerked their heads around and stared at the oncoming Indians.

Keefe didn't try to estimate their numbers, but he knew his guess of a thousand warriors could not have been too far wrong.

Over the screaming din of battle, Keefe heard Burkhalter's roar, "Dismount and fight on foot!" and afterward the cries, "Horse holders!"

All this time a murderous withering hail of bullets had been tearing into the ranks of B and K Troops from the defenders of the village below them on the slope. Men were dropping from one end of the line to the other. But these were veterans, not the kind to panic under attack. The horse holders took the mounts of the dismounted cavalrymen and trotted to the side with them. The men remaining dropped to the ground, taking cover behind dead and wounded horses, some even behind their own dead comrades.

MacPhee saw the Indians on the ridge at the same time Keefe saw them and involuntarily raised a hand to halt his men. They halted and milled uncertainly, while MacPhee tried to decide what he must do in the face of this new and unexpected development.

Keefe understood the dilemma instantly. B and K Troops were pinned down in a murderous crossfire, and time was running out. In minutes, now, the ranks of Indians galloping down from the ridge would reach them and annihilate them.

MacPhee had a decision to make, a desperate and deadly one. He could throw L Troop into the breach, probably sacrificing them in an attempt to rescue B and K. Or he could withdraw L Troop intact and have at least that much. He glanced at Keefe, his eyes tortured with indecision . . .

He was spared the need to decide. Even as his eyes held Keefe's, a bullet struck him in the neck.

It was a heavy slug from an ancient buffalo gun. It shattered his spinal column and tore a hole in his throat nearly as big as a fist. Half severed from his body, his head lolled to one side. Blood drenched the front of his tunic and the head and neck of his horse.

Spooked by the smell, by the wetness of blood that had nearly blinded him, the horse bolted. MacPhee's body slammed limply from side to side with each jump he took.

Horror momentarily stunned the mind of Lieutenant Keefe. He heard only vaguely the savage sounds of battle, the cries of those wounded and in pain. But he snapped out of it before much more than a split second had gone by. MacPhee had been spared the agonising decision that must be made. Responsibility for it now rested on him instead.

Nor was there time to consider carefully. The decision must be made, at once, and implemented immediately.

Standing in his stirrups, Keefe waved his arm forward. His voice was a harsh bellow, carrying down the line of men even above the din of battle, "Clean this damned village out! B and K Troops have got to have cover from that bunch up there!"

Instantly L Troop surged into motion. Into the clustered village the troopers galloped, slashing with sabres, firing pistols, shooting with carbines, and clubbing with them when they were empty.

Behind Keefe and slightly to his right, a trooper was literally driven backward out of his saddle. He struck on his back and the air was expelled violently from his lungs with a sound Keefe could hear even above the shouts and battle sounds. But the man was dead; he had been dead before his body struck the ground. His horse galloped on ahead in terror, turning at the village edge and paralleling the slope as he headed for the trees where the B and K's horse holders had gone previously.

A gun roared almost in Keefe's face, the powder smoke like a heated blast, nearly blinding him. Then his horse's shoulder struck the Indian who had fired it, and flung him aside, and Keefe levelled his revolver and put a bullet into the Indian's chest.

Another Cheyenne brave, face contorted with hatred, leaped at him with a fisted tomahawk. Keefe fired again, and a second time, but this time the hammer clicked down on an empty chamber. He slammed the gun into his holster and swiftly drew his sabre. He slashed at the Indian, coming on again, and saw the blade cut half-way through the Indian's neck.

By now L Troop had, by the very savagery of its attack, demoralised the Indians. The Cheyennes slipped like ghosts between the tipis, heading for the right flank where B and K Troops' horse holders were.

Keefe roared, "Dismount and fight on foot!" and his order was repeated again and again by noncoms who heard it, and those cries were followed by the familiar cries, "Horse holders!"

Back through the village the horse holders led the mounts, while the dismounted troopers reloaded their guns and began firing at the galloping Cheyennes, now scarcely more than a hundred and fifty yards away.

Out there in the open, Burkhalter raised up from behind a dead horse and yelled, "Take cover on the left!" Crouching low, he began to run laterally along the slope in the direction the horse holders had gone earlier.

Keefe had hoped Burkhalter would let his men fall back into the village which L Troop had cleared of Indians. Perhaps Burkhalter did not realise it was clear, he thought, but the major was, by retreating laterally along the slope, leaving L Troop alone to face the murderous charge of the horde of Indians that had appeared minutes before at the crest of the ridge.

No massacre of Indians this, thought Keefe bitterly. Already he had lost a fifth of his command. Burkhalter had lost a third. The bare slope was strewn with dead and dying horses, with wounded men and with dead ones too.

Keefe began to reload his revolver with trembling hands, hoping he could accomplish this awkward task before the howling savages got this far.

Joe Moya was with Burkhalter when the major led B Troop and K out of the creek bottom and up through the brush and trees toward the spine of the low ridge behind the Cheyenne village. He rode beside the major in the strengthening light, his gleaming eyes hidden behind their secretive, slitted lids. In a few more moments Burkhalter was going to know how deadly was the trap that was about to close on him. He was going to begin paying for the massacre at Cut Nose Creek. He was going to see his command cut to ribbons, bleeding and dying on the ground the way he had left the Indians bleeding and dying at Cut Nose Creek. And when he had seen his command decimated, when he had faced the fact that the future held only disgrace and shame for him, then and only then was Moya going to take his life.

He chuckled softly to himself as the two troops rode along the crest of the ridge. The major called, "Left by twos!" and the command was repeated along the line by Captain Leighton and after that by Lieutenant DuBois, "Left by twos!" A moment later, in a slightly louder voice, accompanied by an arm signal, the major gave the command to execute, "Ho-o-o-o!" and immediately after that, "Halt!"

Joe Moya had read the tracks at Cut Nose Creek and he knew this was the same attack plan that had been used there. Burkhalter had come on the village from the rear, in column of twos. He had wheeled the command into line behind the village, and seconds later had ordered the charge. Lieutenant Hargreaves had brought the other force along the creek bottom where MacPhee was now.

Moya found himself thinking of that new lieutenant, Keefe. Keefe had damned near spoiled his plan, first by reaching O'Rourke before the old scout died and afterward by repeating his dying words. Last night he'd nearly spoiled it again by leaving camp and scouting the Indian village. Fortunately,

Burkhalter had been sufficiently intoxicated by the thought of promotion that he had closed his mind to everything Keefe had said.

He realised suddenly that Burkhalter was looking at him. "You don't have to remain, Mr. Moya. You are a civilian and not paid to fight."

Moya said, "I'll stay, Major, if it's all the same to you." He was thinking, "You son-of-a-bitch, you're not going to get rid of me that easily. I want to be around and see what happens to you even if I get killed myself for my pains."

Burkhalter stood in his stirrups suddenly. He drew his sabre, its steel sliding out of the scabbard with its usual, distinctive sound. He raised the sabre above his head and waved it toward the village down below. He roared, "Cha-a-arge!"

Down toward the village swept the line, undulating like some great serpent as it moved. Moya was out in front, trying to angle his horse to the right so that he would be near Major Burkhalter all the time. He wasn't going to be cheated, even by death, he thought grimly. He was going to be near Burkhalter so that even if the major sustained a hit, he would not be able to expire peacefully. Moya meant to do his gloating as the major died, if he was not allowed to do it earlier.

Behind Moya and the major, the command split slightly to right and left, so that neither the scout nor the commanding officer would be in their line of fire. Carbines and pistols cracked along the galloping line of shouting men. But suddenly, from ahead, resistance developed unexpectedly. Steady, deliberate, witheringly accurate fire began to come from the village, from behind tipis, from slits cut in their sides, from behind barricades of piled-up hides and blankets and dried buffalo meat. Two men went down on Moya's left, two more in rapid succession on Burkhalter's right.

Moya, smiling grimly to himself, kept his glance steadily on the major's face. Once or twice he glanced over his shoulder. He saw the first of the massed Cheyennes that appeared from behind the crest of the ridge. He heard their cries and saw the utter consternation in Burkhalter's eyes as the major swung his head to look.

The line of galloping men stopped suddenly. Horses reared and pranced. The men stared at the terrible horde of Indians galloping toward them down the slope. They turned their heads and stared back at the village, from which such deadly fire was pouring into their ranks.

Already their casualties were frightening. Twenty — thirty — forty men were down. Loose horses milled around, undecided as to which way to run. A couple of horses lay kicking on the ground. One was nickering shrilly, sounding like an old woman screaming with intolerable pain.

Burkhalter looked at Moya. Moya grinned mockingly at him. The major, his face suddenly turning grey, snatched for his pistol. He raised it, pointed it at Moya, and pulled the trigger. The gun fired but the bullet missed. He had no opportunity to fire a second time. Men and horses boiled between the two, obscuring each from the other one.

Moya realised he was screaming almost hysterically at Burkhalter even though he knew the man couldn't hear. "You bastard! You murderin' son-of-a-bitch! You killed them! You killed my family! Now by God you're gettin' a little of the same!"

He heard Burkhalter's roaring voice, even though he could not see the man. "Dismount and fight on foot!" and afterward the cries that ran along the line, "Horse holders!"

Moya's horse caught a bullet in the neck and went down, forequarters first. Moya stepped out of the saddle, trying to decide on which side of the horse's body he should take cover.

He stared toward the village through the blue-hazy cloud of powder smoke. He saw the men of L Troop coming through. He saw the Indian defenders fading away singly among the tipis, heading in the direction B and K Troops' horse holders were taking the horses, toward the trees. He dropped down behind his horse between the horse's body and the village down below.

He had no weapon in his hands. He had no intention of killing Indians, even to save his life. He stared around, keeping his head down, looking for Burkhalter but not seeing him.

At the village, the men of L Troop began to fire at the galloping wave of Indians sweeping wildly down from the crest of the ridge. Their bullets must be less than a dozen feet overhead, thought Moya, keeping his head low instinctively.

Not Burkhalter. Either the major lost his head and panicked or he did not realise that L Troop had taken the village. He leaped up from behind a dead horse, covered with dust and blood, hat gone, and yelled, "Take cover on the left!"

Moya thought, "You damned fool! Your

only chance was down below in the village with L Troop and now you've thrown that chance away." But this was what he wanted. He wanted to see the force from Fort Kettering annihilated, killed to the last blue-coated man. Only then could he truly feel that Red Earth Woman and the children had been avenged.

CHAPTER 19

Keefe watched the remnants of B and K Troops running laterally along the slope in response to Burkhalter's command. He knew that now his own L Troop had no chance, no chance at all. That galloping line of savages would reach the village edge in a matter of seconds, a minute or two at most. There would be a score of Indians against each trooper . . .

Damn it, he wasn't going to let his men be slaughtered that way. He'd brought them in here to save Burkhalter and he wasn't going to let them be murdered for their pains.

Oblivious of the bullets tearing into the tipis around him, he leaped out into the open, his back to the Indians coming down the ridge. He roared, "Take cover! Take cover to the right!"

His sabre was in his hand. He waved it toward the trees along the creek into which Burkhalter's men had all but disappeared. There was damned little cover in those trees against the hundreds of Indians that would be besieging them, but it was the best cover available. And at least the command would not be split into two separate contingents. At least they'd all be together when they died.

And die they would. He could see no alternative. They were outnumbered at least five to one. They were demoralised because they had been led into a trap.

Keefe held back, herding his men ahead of him the way a herder does his sheep. The sound of galloping hooves was louder now, a growing thunder in the air. It was dust, and powder smoke, and the hot smell of blood, and of horses, and of the Indian camp itself. The men were running ahead of him, running for their lives and knowing it, and Keefe was staying close at their heels, his breath growing short, his back aching in expectation of an arrow, or lance, or bullet striking it.

They rolled over him like a tide. A horse struck him and knocked him tumbling for more than twenty feet. He clung to his sabre, and got up and sprinted for the brush and trees again.

That charge slamming into the tail-enders of L Troop had left a dozen of them lying dead. Keefe caught the blue of their uniforms from the corner of his eye as he plunged frantically for the cover of the brush and trees still nearly fifty yards away.

Again he heard the thunder of hooves coming on behind. He threw a quick glance over his shoulder. A savage was coming after him, tomahawk in hand, leading far out in order to make his kill.

Keefe flung himself forward at the last instant, sliding prone along the ground. The Indian horseman went past, and a volley of fire cracked from the screen of brush. Keefe got up and ran on, seeing the emptied saddle of the Indian's horse, seeing the dead Indian lying on the ground.

He reached the brush and trees and plunged into them, tripping and sprawling out headlong. Instantly there were half a dozen men of L Troop there, ready to help him up. They had saved his life by turning and covering him, but there was no time to think about that now. He looked around for Burkhalter. Not seeing him, he roared, "Cover this side! Shoot from a prone position! Any of you that don't have guns start throwing up barricades!"

The men jumped to obey him, not only those from L Troop but the men from B and K as well. Keefe took a position behind a tree and began to reload his revolver again.

The village on the bank of Rialto Creek was like an anthill someone had just stirred with a stick. Mounted, milling savages were everywhere. A few of them fired without plan into the brush and trees where the hated pony soldiers were. In minutes, though, they'd form up again, rallied by their chiefs. They'd charge the thicket and that would be the end of it.

Keefe turned his head and shouted, "Major! Major Burkhalter!" He received no reply, so he shouted, "Captain Leighton! Lieutenant DuBois!"

A trooper, limping on a wounded, bloody leg, came to him. "Captain Leighton's dead, sir. Lieutenant DuBois caught a bullet in the shoulder and he's unconscious, sir. Dr. Lynch is working on him now."

"Where's Major Burkhalter?"

"Over there, sir." The trooper gestured vaguely with a hand.

Keefe finished loading his revolver. He walked in the direction the trooper had indicated and, after travelling through the brush for a couple of dozen yards, saw Burkhalter sitting on a fallen tree. He stopped and stared. Burkhalter did not seem to be aware of what was going on around him. He did not seem aware of the dilemma his command was in. Moya stood nearby, staring at Burkhalter with hate-filled, triumphant eyes. For a moment Keefe considered shooting Moya dead. While he hesitated, he heard the Indians in the village begin yelling in unison again.

He whirled and ran back that way, shouting as he did, "Cover this side, troopers! Come on, damn you, we're not dead yet!"

Those at the edge of the little brush pocket began to fire at the charging Indians. Keefe raised his revolver, sighted carefully, and squeezed off a shot. He was rewarded by seeing an Indian tumble from his saddle. He steadied the gun for the next shot against the trunk of a scrub cottonwood and again saw his target fall.

Screaming, howling, they came on, but they pulled up at the edge of the brush pocket and veered away at right angles to it. Others behind them came on, also veering aside at the last instant. The firing seemed to go on for ever. Keefe's gun was empty. He was standing ready with his sabre in his hand when the last of the screaming savages galloped away after the rest.

Keefe shouted, "Reload! They'll be back!"

and began to reload his revolver, the barrel of which was almost too hot to touch. Around him the men were reloading hastily, with fingers that shook violently as they worked. Keefe saw two that didn't move. Another was groaning with pain. Still another sat staring at blood welling out of a hole in his thigh, his face white with shock.

Keefe shouted, "Surgeon! Dr. Lynch!"

His gun reloaded, he stepped away from the edge of the thicket, saying as he did, "Take charge here, Sergeant Hochstadt."

"Yes, sir." Hochstadt was a steady one, Keefe thought. He seemed as unperturbed as though he were on the firing range. Or perhaps it was only fatalism. Perhaps Hochstadt knew he was dead, and had decided there was nothing to get perturbed about any more.

Keefe walked slowly through the thicket, among the men remaining from Troops B and L and K. The sun slanted warmly through the leaves overhead, dappling the ground with shade. He glanced up at the sky with amazement. The sun was hardly up. It had been less than half an hour since he first led L Troop splashing along the creek. Now MacPhee was dead, and Leighton. DuBois was unconscious and Burkhalter was apparently suffering from shock.

He walked the perimeter of the thicket in which they had taken cover. A picket line had been set up for the horses near the creek. Three of them were down, killed by bullets tearing through the thicket during the last Indian attack.

All around the thicket, men were working feverishly, throwing up barricades. Keefe stared at the horses, scowling to himself. If he left them here on the picket line they would all, ultimately, be killed. The smell of them would permeate the area, making every breath unbearable. He knew he ought to have them cut loose and driven off.

But he shook his head reluctantly. The morale of the men was bad enough without making it any worse. The horses were the only chance they had of cheating death. Not a man here but knew they couldn't fight their way out of this. Without horses, they'd know they had no chance even to escape.

Several resourceful troopers had taken sabres from dead comrades, snapped them off a foot from the hilt, and were now using them to dig entrenchments facing the open country toward the village and toward the ridge. Once the ground had been loosened by the men with the broken sabres, other men pushed it forward with their hands, forming low barricades. Keefe saw Dr.

Lynch working frantically with the wounded, giving crisp orders to the men he had pressed into service to help.

So far, nobody'd had time to give much thought to how grim their situation was. They had no food. The only ammunition they had was what each man carried for himself. At least half the men were casualties, dead or too badly wounded to fight.

Keefe walked the edge of the thicket, staring toward the Indians already regrouping near the crest of the ridge. His mind was like a squirrel in a cage, probing, seeking, searching for some way out. But there wasn't any way. There wasn't any way out but death.

Moya stood leaning against a tree, staring with angry disgust at Major Burkhalter. The major seemed to be suffering from shock.

Despite his anger and disgust, shock was something Joe Moya could understand. It was something he had experienced himself, and not too long ago. He'd been numb with it when he first saw the burning village on Cut Nose Creek, with the bodies strewn so carelessly around. He'd been all but unable to function for a long time after he found Red Earth Woman lying dead, and the children also dead on the other side of the burning lodge.

Burkhalter had sustained a shock of equal intensity, he supposed. Only in the major's case he hadn't lost a wife and children. He'd lost a dream. He'd lost the force that motivated his life.

The major had been so sure — that this attack would go off as smoothly and as murderously as had the one on Cut Nose Creek . . . Moya continued to stare at Burkhalter, hating him, yet feeling triumphant too. He had avenged his wife and children. He had ruined Burkhalter. He had delivered the pony soldiers from Fort Kettering into the hands of the Cheyennes. Half of them were already casualties. The other half would be dead soon.

He didn't even think of his own safety. He didn't, honestly, care whether he lived or died. In the long run at least. He just wanted to stay alive long enough to see Burkhalter's ruin complete.

Keefe came looking for Burkhalter, saw how he was and went away. The Cheyennes attacked again, in wave after wave, veering off at the edge of the thicket, escaping with light losses and riding out of range to regroup before coming in again. They were in no hurry to end the fighting here. They could afford to take their time. The pony soldiers were not going to get away.

Burkhalter continued to stare straight ahead of him unseeingly. Moya walked over and sat down beside him on the fallen tree. He said softly, "Can you hear me, Major? Can you hear me, you bloody son-of-a-bitch?"

His first question elicited no response. The second brought a dull flush to Burkhalter's face. Moya chuckled. "You understand that, don't you, you lousy, stinkin' bastard? Well listen good, you maggot, because there's something I want you to hear."

Burkhalter's face held its dull flush. His eyes had narrowed slightly. He can hear all right, Moya thought. He can hear if I make him hear. He said, "Keefe was right about what O'Rourke said before he died. O'Rourke told me that same thing and that's why I had to stick my knife in him."

Burkhalter turned his head. He stared at Moya unbelievingly.

Moya chuckled softly. "Don't look so surprised. Because here's something that will really surprise you, you son-of-a-bitch. I planned this ambush. When you sent me out to scout I went up north of Cut Nose Creek to Tall Elk's village. I told him to locate this dummy camp here on Rialto Creek. I gave him time to pull every Cheyenne buck into it that he could find."

There was understanding in the major's eyes now. His lips formed the words, "Why? For God's sake, why?"

"My family was there at Cut Nose Creek." Moya put his face close to Burkhalter's and spat the words at him. "My family was there and when I got back that day I found them dead, my wife and my son and my little girl. I carried them out and I buried them and I swore on their graves that I'd get you and the men that did your dirty work."

Burkhalter was coming out of it now. His hand went to his side, groping numbly for his revolver. Anger came into his eyes.

Moya said softly, "Go ahead, Major. Grab your lousy gun. But before you get it out I'll have this knife buried in your gut!"

Burkhalter stopped his hand. He brought it out in front of him and let it rest upon his knee. His face was grey now, all the blood having ebbed out of it. His eyes were dead, without hope. Moya said softly, "So your chance of ever makin' general is gone, ain't it, Major? You're going to have to stay here in this stinkin' little thicket and watch your men killed off one by one until they're gone. I hope you're last, Major. I hope the Cheyennes take you alive. They don't generally torture prisoners but I reckon they'd make an exception in your case. And if they won't,

I will. I'd like to see you die real slow. Screamin' like a woman, Major. Beggin' to be killed."

Burkhalter raised his head. He opened his mouth to call out, but Moya said softly, "Don't, Major. I can have a knife in you before anybody even knows what you want."

Burkhalter turned his head and stared steadily into Moya's eyes. He was grey and without hope, but there was suddenly a quality in his eyes that had not been there before. He opened his mouth and shouted suddenly, "Lieutenant Keefe! I want this man placed under arrest! And if he tries to escape, I want him shot!"

For an instant surprise held Moya still. Burkhalter raised his voice again, "Lieutenant Keefe!"

Moya said softly, "All right, you son-of-a-bitch. You asked for it. By God, I hope it hurts." He put the point of his knife against the straining cloth of Burkhalter's tunic and pushed it home.

Burkhalter's breath gusted out in a high "Ah-h-h!" of pain. Moya withdrew the knife, getting casually to his feet. He saw Keefe coming. He saw Sergeant Hochstadt coming behind him. Neither man seemed to realise what had happened.

Moya strode swiftly away, not sure but

what they'd shoot him in the back. He reached the picket line and untied the nearest horse. He swung to the saddle, took to the water, and spurred the horse savagely.

Behind him, belatedly, he heard the rapid firing of Keefe's revolver. But he was clear. All he had to worry about now was the Indians.

CHAPTER 20

Keefe shoved his smoking revolver into its holster. He knelt beside Burkhalter, who had doubled over and was now hugging himself as if he had a bellyache. Keefe asked urgently, "What is it, sir? What is it?"

Burkhalter only groaned. Keefe raised his head, glanced around, and shouted, "Dr. Lynch! Quickly!"

Lynch, his hands bloody, his face sweating copiously, came hurrying toward him. Keefe said, "It's the major, sir. I don't know . . ."

The surgeon put his hands on Burkhalter's shoulders to straighten him. Burkhalter's face was ghastly now and he seemed to have no strength. Blood had soaked the front of his tunic, had soaked both legs and both arms and hands. Lynch said, "Help me to lay him down. I don't know . . ."

Between them they got the major

stretched out on the ground. Burkhalter had lost consciousness and his eyes were closed. His usually florid skin looked like grey wax. His chest rose and fell rapidly but shallowly. Lynch looked up and shook his head. "I'm afraid he's a goner, Lieutenant Keefe. I'll do what I can, of course, but . . ."

Keefe nodded. He stared down at Burkhalter's face a moment more, then turned away. He wondered why he didn't feel cheated. He had wanted some kind of vengeance against Burkhalter. It had been the reason for his coming to Fort Kettering. Now Burkhalter was going to die leaving him unsatisfied.

He walked slowly back to the earth and brush breastworks the men had thrown up, reloading his revolver as he did. In a round-about way, he supposed, his father *had* been avenged by Burkhalter's ultimate defeat. Defeat was the one thing Burkhalter had not been able to tolerate. Defeat had broken him and if it culminated in his death that was only incidental to the defeat itself.

He'd had his vengeance but he guessed he'd wanted more than simple vengeance against the man. Smiling ruefully to himself, he supposed what he had really wanted was for Burkhalter to publicly admit jumping the gun at Indian Creek. That could never happen now. It was doubtful if Burkhalter was ever going to regain consciousness.

It was unimportant anyway. What mattered now was the desperate situation of these men. There seemed no way out for them, no way out but death. It was certain they couldn't defeat the Indians. Nor could they fight their way back to Fort Kettering.

Keefe walked to where Sergeant Hochstadt was. Hochstadt said, "They've got a powwow going on up there, Lieutenant. I reckon some of 'em, the hotheads likely, want to overrun us and get it over with. The cooler heads want to hold back and starve us out. They don't like the losses they've been taking every time they charge."

Keefe glanced up at the crest of the ridge. The Indians were milling around up there. A small group of the older ones stood together on the ground facing the younger, mounted ones, who yelled and gesticulated excitedly.

Keefe said, "We're finished if we don't get word back to the fort."

"We're finished anyhow. There's only half a troop at Fort Kettering. They wouldn't be any help."

"There's help at Fort Laramie and at Reno and at Fort Kearney and at Fort Fred Steele. There's help at Omaha, if we can get to the telegraph and if the lines aren't down."

Hochstadt grinned. "That's a lot of ifs, Lieutenant Keefe. But I'll go if you want me to."

"I won't order you . . ."

"Hell, Lieutenant, what difference does it make? We'll all be dead anyhow. What does it matter how or where?"

Keefe nodded. "All right, Hochstadt. Now listen to me. You've got to outrun those Indians and there's only one way you can do it. Take three horses. When they begin to gain on you, change horses and leave the played out one behind. The two extra ones won't wear down so quickly if they're not carrying any weight."

"Yes, sir. When do you want me to go?"

"Right now would be a good time, Hochstadt. While they're busy arguing about what they're going to do."

Hochstadt got up. He stared at Keefe for a moment before he said hesitantly, "It was wrong, what we did to them at Cut Nose Creek, Lieutenant Keefe. I guess I can't blame 'em much for what they're doin' to us now."

Keefe nodded. "Get going, Sergeant. Take the three best horses on the line."

The sergeant strode away. Keefe glanced

back at the ridge where the Indians were still arguing. He hoped they'd keep on arguing for a little longer. He walked toward the picket line.

Hochstadt had three horses picked out by the time he arrived. He tied one of the spares to the tail of the other. Holding that one's reins, he mounted and saluted easily. "Good luck, Lieutenant."

"Same to you, Hochstadt."

Hochstadt rode along the edge of the stream cautiously, hoping to get a little distance away before he was discovered, Keefe supposed. But he didn't get far. Keefe heard a high yell, and a shot, and then Hochstadt dug in his spurs and thundered out of sight.

Instantly a volley of shots sounded out there. Keefe held his breath. If those guns stopped shooting suddenly it would mean Hochstadt was down.

But they did not stop and Keefe's breath sighed slowly out. Hochstadt had got clear. Now if he could just stay clear . . .

The Cheyennes sent in an attacking party of forty or fifty just then, yelling crazily. Two of them got clear through, into the grove of trees. Keefe shot one of them. The other was riddled from behind.

After that, except for sniper fire, it was

quiet for a long, long time. The sun climbed across the sky, reached its zenith, and dropped toward the horizon in the west. The wounded groaned and talked deliriously, and occasionally one of them yelled with pain. Lynch and the men helping him worked incessantly. They had no bandages, those Lynch had brought with him in his saddlebags having long since been used up. Lynch made do with strips torn from shirts.

Burkhalter, amazingly, lingered until late afternoon. When he died it was silently, without having regained consciousness. Keefe found himself wishing it had not been so easy for Burkhalter. He wished the major could have stayed alive and seen what his ambition had done to the men of his command.

In late afternoon, right after Burkhalter died, Keefe ordered one of the horses killed, ordered the men to butcher it. They skinned and quartered it and hung the meat in the trees to cool.

At sundown, the Cheyennes sent in another charge but it was a half-hearted one that veered aside before it got closer than a hundred yards. After that, until it was completely dark, the Cheyennes contented themselves with sporadic sniping.

Keefe had sentries posted behind the barricades and ordered the remaining men to rest and sleep. He had a pit dug, and a fire built in it, and a quarter of horsemeat put on a spit over it. Occasionally a bullet slammed into the pit, but no one was hit.

Now that there was nothing more to be done, Keefe discovered that he was exhausted. It had been the longest day of his life, and the hardest. It was probably the last full day he would know. To-morrow at this time he would probably be dead.

If it weren't for the wounded, he thought, he could make an attempt to mount the men and run for it. As it was, there was nothing they could do but wait and fight until the end.

The night dragged by. Keefe slept only lightly, awakening often at some small noise. While it was yet half an hour before dawn, he sent the sentries around the beleaguered little compound to waken the men. In the chill before the dawn, they slashed chunks off the quarter of horsemeat and wolfed them down. They filled their canteens at the creek. Then they took their places grimly behind the barricades, each facing the coming of this day differently, but facing it.

Two or three of them had bad cases of the shakes, Keefe noticed. Some were very pale. Universally they were silent, speaking only when it was necessary and then in muted whispers.

Gradually the line of grey along the eastern horizon strengthened. Gradually objects became visible in the growing light. Keefe could not help remembering yesterday morning and the wild ride up the course of Rialto Creek into what he knew was going to be a trap.

Scowling with concentration, he tried to pierce the grey dawn light with his eyes. He knew a charge would come. He wanted to know from what direction it would come in time to shift the bulk of his troopers to that side.

A breeze stirred in the south, blowing along the course of Rialto Creek. The smell of sagebrush, crushed by the hooves of the Indian ponies, was pungent, strong. Juices from the quarter of horsemeat on the spit sizzled as they dropped onto the bed of coals beneath. A trooper lighted his last cigar, savouring its taste, the smoke pleasant and somehow comforting as it drifted to where Keefe stood.

And then, on the stillness came the distant, muted yipping of the Indians as they began their charge. The sounds seemed to come from all directions, not from a single one. Keefe shouted, "Hold your fire until they're close enough. Don't shoot until you're sure you're going to hit something."

It was almost eerie, those muted sounds coming out of the grey mists of dawn. Then, on the heels of the shrill cries of the Cheyennes, came the low rumble of thunder from their massed horses' hooves. "They'll overrun us this time," Keefe thought, as he thumbed back the hammer of his army Colt.

Staring out toward the crest of the ridge from which the attacks had come yesterday, he was suddenly able to discern movement, and then individuals, and lastly the depth of the charge, the almost horrifying proportions of it. The line of charging Indians stretched from the creek to the crest of the ridge, and along that, and back down to the creek on the other side. He turned his head and peered through the brush and trees in the direction of the picket line. He could see them coming from that direction too, their horses' hooves raising a high cloud of spray as they pounded into the creek. They had planned this dawn attack last night and were putting everything they had into it. In one charge they would even the score for Cut Nose Creek, and more.

Keefe shouted, "Hold your fire! Hold your fire!" as two troopers fired wildly at the advancing line. The rest of the troopers waited, staring with fascination at the Indians.

The Indians were close now, closer than a hundred yards. Keefe roared, "All right! Pick your target and fire!" Instantly a volley rattled out and a cloud of powder smoke swept along the thinned line of cavalrymen.

Horses somersaulted and crashed to the ground, throwing their riders as much as thirty feet. Saddles were suddenly empty, the horses coming on without direction, caught up in the excitement of it, pushed on remorselessly from behind.

A second volley rattled out, more scattered than the first. Again horses came crashing to the ground and braves were driven out of their saddles. But the toll of the troopers' carbines seemed to make no difference. The screaming, painted, barbaric line of horsemen came on unchecked.

Keefe fired now, with the Indians well within the range of his revolver. He knocked one brave out of his saddle and put a bullet into the shoulder of another one. His third shot downed a horse. His fourth brought a rush of blood from the throat of an oldster with a magnificent warbonnet whipping out behind his head.

Then it was hand to hand, with the Indians' horses jumping the barricades, or crashing through them, or stopping abruptly at their edge, the riders coming on afoot. Keefe stood with his back to a tree and put his last shot into a running Indian, afterward throwing the revolver straight into the Indian's face.

He drew his sabre and hacked a scarlet slash in the chest of still another Indian. The sound of battle rolled over him, deafening, bringing the memory of other sounds from the dim recesses of the past, the sound of bugles trumpeting the charge, cavalry bugles sounding the stirringly familiar call . . .

Suddenly he raised his head, frozen for an instant with disbelief. Those sounds had not come out of his memory of the past. Those sounds were real.

Real too was the way the Indians pulled back out of the screaming mêlée, real the way they galloped, or ran afoot, back up the slopes from which they had come only moments earlier.

Keefe had a bullet hole clean through his shoulder, which was burning like fire and bleeding copiously. Blood dripped from his sabre's blade. Two dead Indians and a wounded one lay at his feet.

But the Cheyennes were gone, and behind them, driving them, galloped a long line of cavalrymen. Keefe leaned against the tree weakly. He saw a group of officers ride up beyond the barricades. He heard Sergeant Hochstadt's voice call out, "Lieutenant Keefe? You all right, sir?"

One of the mounted officers wore the twin stars of a major general on the front of his dusty campaign hat. Keefe stared at him, recognising him as General Stiles, Commander of the Department of the Platte, from Omaha. He had no idea how the general could have got here this soon, or even how he had got here at all.

He began to feel light-headed and very weak. His knees were like water. He put out a hand and touched the trunk of the scrubby tree to steady himself . . .

He was falling, falling . . . It seemed as though he fell for ever. But he had no recollection of striking the ground.

All of that day, the troops from Fort Kettering and those of the relief column remained on Rialto Creek while they burned their dead, cared for their wounded, and rested those of Burkhalter's command who had sustained no wounds.

Keefe slept the entire day, and the night following. He awoke for the first time in a jolting ambulance early on the morning of the second day.

Memories of that last bloody charge by the Cheyennes came flooding back. He was surprised to find himself alive.

He sat up carefully, bracing himself against the sides of the ambulance. Lieutenant DuBois lay beside him and beside DuBois was a trooper, face bandaged so that Keefe was unable to recognise him. Dr. Lynch sat near the tail gate of the wagon looking at him.

Keefe grinned faintly. "They arrived just in time, didn't they?"

The surgeon returned his grin. "They sure as hell did."

"How did they get there so soon? Hochstadt couldn't have . . ."

"Hochstadt didn't. He met them between Rialto Creek and Fort Kettering. Seems the general had a hunch Burkhalter would disobey orders and go out glory hunting. So he headed out for Fort Kettering the same day the telegraph wires were cut."

Keefe nodded. He felt strangely at peace to-day, as though something that had hung over his head a long, long time was there no more.

No longer did he need reassurance that his father had been in the right at Indian Creek during the war. It surprised him now that there had ever been any doubt in his mind.

He lay back and closed his eyes. The jolting went on and on interminably. He hoped he would be allowed to remain at Fort Kettering. There was an abiding affection in him for this regiment that he knew would never fade. And now, his life could go forward with neither uncertainty nor the hunger for revenge to sour it. The battle of Indian Creek had been buried with the body of Major Burkhalter and so had the Cut Nose Massacre.

The employees of Thorndike Press hope you have enjoyed this Large Print book. All our Thorndike, Wheeler, and Kennebec Large Print titles are designed for easy reading, and all our books are made to last. Other Thorndike Press Large Print books are available at your library, through selected bookstores, or directly from us.

For information about titles, please call:
  (800) 223-1244

or visit our Web site at:
  http://gale.cengage.com/thorndike

To share your comments, please write:
  Publisher
  Thorndike Press
  10 Water St., Suite 310
  Waterville, ME 04901